LONDON CALLING

Wayne Wignall

www.waynewignall.com

ISBN Paperback: 978-1-63323-391-1

PROLOGUE

IT RAN, IN her mind, what was going to happen as two masked men stood right in front of her. She couldn't believe that her husband was slumped beside her as well.

"My little girl Alice," one of them, in a well-spoken accent, patronised, "you do understand why we're here, don't you?"

"Yes!" Alice cried in a panic.

He pointed at the dead body. "He should have warned you that we cannot allow that diary to get published," he said. "And there's that other arsehole who should've told you of the dangers to make that attempt. You only wanted to make money out of something you've no appreciation of."

Alice couldn't accept that she was going to die; she was a ghost writer of a renowned publishing house that named and shamed the corrupt. She also had a reputation of being rewarded the title as Dame for her work. Now, she was bound onto a chair, by two thugs, who were telling her exactly the same details before they killed her husband. The man that had patronised her took a seat; the only sound heard was the chair being rubbed by his leather coat and he liked it. Perhaps it was familiar to him yet not really pleasing to comprehend — dare I say that it was synthetic to a purring cat. He was still adjusting in his seat to find his comfort until he nodded with both of his hands on the arm rests. There was a staircase which would twirl from the left hand corner, and it had astounded him from his earlier examination that the entire railing was made of marble. The intruder sensed a pleasure of either going up, or down it: To the bedroom to complete "his" evening, or welcome a brand new day. As well as that, he was staggered to see that there weren't any paintings or photographs on display anywhere. The wall ahead of him was covered in darkly varnished bamboo stems: Upright and unevenly spread. They even cast shadows as the only light in the room was coming from the laminated wall. The unwelcomed guest saw reading square-lamps nearby all of the chairs too that evening. To his left, a huge window was fitted from the foot to the ceiling. Oddly enough, there wasn't a way to vent air except a control panel to turn on the air conditioning. He gasped in wonder before looking at the ceiling: Concave with spotlights in a single file. There was something cooking; the smell invited and teased him to get up to follow his nose. His entrance was just as astonishing as the room he left: A chandelier was hanging above it. The kitchen was mainly white except for the stools and table. The man remained dazzled by the yellow bar of light that lit along the edges at the bottom. As if unorthodox, there were pictures and a clock on the walls. Anyway, his curiosity led him nearer to the cooker and turned it off before taking a taste from the saucepan; the impertinent gentleman could taste the lobster in the soup. After all that, he re-emerged into the living room.

"Alice," he said getting close to her, "you've a remarkable home. This place of yours is honestly earned. I do have great regards—"

"Is it money that you want?"

The gentleman was quite prodigious as he stared at her. He shook his head and was putting his hands on his knees to lean forward. He laughed. "Have you lost your mind? If I wanted money, do you think I would have shot your husband without asking first? Of course not! I believe in our ideal world," he said. "But," he asked sarcastically, "you're a pig so you're going to die, yes?"

Why should Alice answer him, he brought no warmth since forcing himself into her home. She closed her eyes.

"That's a good girl, Alice." He stoked her hair but pulled on it. "How would you like to die?"

Die and for what? Alice asked herself. She hadn't done anything wrong and knew that that *diary* would've been big. She had written on behalf of people that wanted to make a difference on love-rats; mischievous charities and celebrity rapists. Beforehand, nobody dared to cross her — even the media too.

"What are you thinking about mad 'am?" he asked and was pointing the shotgun right into her face.

"Please I must understand, why are you doing this?"

"Aren't you the forgetful one?" he seemed to ask. "That *diary* is slander and it mustn't go out into the open. Now do you understand?"

"But you could've told us—"

"That is exactly what we're doing now! But you aren't the type that listens to obnoxious people, are you?"

"I'm listening now!"

The man smirked. "You listen because you haven't a choice."

There was a third person in the lounge held against his will. He watched haplessly as his Ghost-writer and Agent were gone. It was his turn now as they were going to justify their actions why he must be damned too.

"Clive Roberts, isn't it?"

"You must know,' Clive answered, "that what you're doing is wrong, don't you?"

The man laughed at him. "Listen here; arsehole," he went on, "do you really think that you're in the position to be philippic? You will be blamed for these murders, do you understand?"

"You think the police are wretched, don't you?"

Sinister as he was, he smiled. "Do I think the police are wretched? You may have the odd one, right? Anyhow, it was you that was holding this gun."

He raised the weapon in full view of his captive and aimed it at him. Still sniggering, he placed the gun onto the table nearby. The hooded man proceeded to carefully remove his latex gloves too. "This is just too easy."

Clive knew he was taunting him — after all, the intruder had all the time in the world to do ill on him. Beforehand, he was vehement and aware of the perils of going public. But all he could do now was watch that man move towards him with his carefully removed gloves.

"Put these on."

"No I will not!"

He grinned. The monster moved across the room looking at an ornament before putting on a clean pair of pvc gloves and returned back. "Must I knock some sense into you?"

"You will not force me to—"

"Don't you see what has just happened in this room? Two people lay dead by gunshot wounds to the head. They haven't a head left, don't you see."

Clive looked at the corpses; they were hardly recognizable. He turned away to close his eyes, trying not to comprehend, in fear of their taste for violence.

The man laughed again. "I said look at them and do look at them properly!" he said before slapping him across his cheek, forcing his head to turn too. "Look!" he shouted again.

Clive was crying before opening his eyes; the people he once knew by their smiles and laughter was now unbelievable. Their heads seemed to have enlarged and was coloured crimson. He couldn't help himself thinking that both Alice and her husband each had two deformed heads, and few teeth. Worse still, he saw their mouths had lost their gentle smiles. Of course, blood and flesh were everywhere. Clive saw some of their blood splattered on his shirt and on his hands. Even his ears were ringing from the two gun blasts. He dared to dream that he wanted to reach for their shotgun and claim their execrable lives—

"Look man," Clive said. "What you believe in is a farce. It doesn't take into account any appreciation on humanity. It's unchristian for Christ sake!"

"Oh really? Just like the Christian cults. I've heard stories of them going against the world and saying exactly what you're proclaiming. But look how they've killed thousands of people in their beliefs of finding the higher being."

"Oh the Lord will show pity on your soul even if you're truly wicked — I'm finding this just too difficult to accept on what you've done this evening."

The man shrugged his shoulders, and waved his removed gloves at Clive. "Save your rap," he said sternly. "You will put these on."

"I'll not be induced anymore and you'll not force me to—"

Clive became more receptive to the men. He couldn't keep this mind in check after a blow across the head. Before he could regain his thoughts, the man made him wear those gloves inside-out that was slippery, wet too. Then he was whacked again.

"This is just far too easy!" he reaffirmed to his associate as he took those gloves off Clive and placed the candle holder into Alice's hand.

CHAPTER 1

OSCAR BROOKS WAS jotting down on what was occurring in front of him; he had already been amazed on the amount of details obtained. It was hot gossip and the revelations at the Old Bailey were out-of-this-world. It was also the final day of the trail of Clive Roberts, and the Jury had already reached their verdict: Guilty. The Judge was passing his sentence:

"Clive Roberts, you've been found guilty on all counts for the murders of Dame Alice Hopper and her husband, Max Hopper, at their home last autumn. You'll answer to your heinous crimes by serving the maximum sentence that the law of this land allows me to give. You'll serve the minimum of thirty-five years without parole in a maximum security prison. It's pretty horrific why you killed them because they decided not to publish your work. Then you decide to turn this court into a circus that an apparition took their lives! You should have known that this court determines hard evidence like the blood under your finger nails. Therefore, you're the perpetrator!" He rose, pointed at Clive Roberts, and instructed others to take him out of his sight.

Oscar rose like everybody else in the court room. From his observation, he was pretty certain that Clive Roberts was the killer and a madman — it was very strange considering that Clive had a career as a British Ambassador in Greece. Clive's Defence Barrister was staring at him; he surely wanted his attention than anybody else around him. Oscar knew him well and delineated that he would be waiting outside in the lobby. He tried moving ahead but people seemed to be rushing in front of him. Oscar knew that most of the people in the room were news correspondents and were trying to leave quickly to make their own reports. Brooks wasn't in the rush since he was going to see his friend. Of course, trying to exit was close to impossible as people were still cutting in front of him. Nearby, he heard somebody crying. She was all alone sitting quietly in her seat; a young woman with long blonde hair was wearing a black dress. She was quite attractive to admire and Oscar felt sorry that she had lost her family in the shotgun murders. He wanted to show his kindness but the barrister was waiting for him. *Maybe next time,* he thought. His heart missed a beat as he gasped. He saw another group of persons clustering close together at the other side of the gallery. *The victims' family,* he now thought, *so the stunning girl was the murderer's daughter?* Regardless, he made his exit to look for

11

Sebastian. After arriving into the lobby, he was the only person standing there. Shortly afterwards, Oscar saw him approaching and his friend had taken off his wig and cloak.

"I think that we ought to go across several streets from here. Just give me fifteen minutes to have a word with Clive Roberts."

"Time is money —"

"But it will be worth it, trust me."

***

Their entrance wasn't noticed as there was hardly anybody. If a pin had dropped, it could have been heard provided that the television, perched above the bar, wasn't on. It was dimly lit creating small white circles upon the floor. Oscar was rubbing his nose when he registered a cleaning agent: Bleach. It made him unsettled to stay since he considered it mainly used for lavatories. Anyway, Sebastian encouraged him to take another step forward as he proceeded ahead. Oscar wiped his feet and was courteous to his offer. Every step had a spring since the carpet was newly fitted and wasn't trodden upon often. Oscar looked at the carpet closely and a pattern was visible: Mainly red with green and yellow dots scattered across it. He looked up and Sebastian was already at the bar waiting to be served.

"Where are people?" Oscar casually asked him.

"It's usually quiet during the day. In the evening, I think it gets jam-packed," he replied cordially.

A bar-attendant came across and Sebastian ordered a pint of cider and his friend's favourite drink: Newcastle Brown. Oscar didn't know where to sit yet again Sebastian beckoned him to follow his lead to the other end of the pub. The pair climbed a short set of steps before placing their drinks on a table.

"That has to be the weirdest court case that I've ever came across since taking up journalism," Oscar said.

"He's guilty and he knows it," Sebastian stated.

"Why did you have to represent him?"

"Have you lost your tiny mind? I'd represented him before at the European Courts in Luxembourg."

"Vaguely," he responded.

"OK," Sebastian said, "I was hired to defend his actions on terminating a former staff of his at the British Embassy. He now wanted to re-hire me for the English Crown Court — that isn't really my expertise. I'll confess that money is the incentive."

"Well, he did make it worse on himself," Oscar said anyway.

"Such a damn bloody fool, did you know that he told me that—"

"I was in the court room all of this time. I know he said some fucking crazy shit that he was *innocent* and *nothing made him do it*!"

"That's exactly what I'm talking about! What the fuck was he on?"

Oscar wanted to smoke his electric cigarette and was looking around if anybody was watching him. He made do with it. "I cannot understand what a psychopath like that had running in his mind. He had an excellent career in Greece but decides to call it a day...Then he wants to publish a diary about his former employees...What the hell is wrong with him?"

Sebastian knocked on the table. "Just because you think that you're a Geordie doesn't give you the right to smoke that crafty cigarette," he said jokingly.

Oscar laughed slightly. "Yeah," he placed the object into his pocket, "that man is just weird."

"I think I should have relinquished that man for he will cause so much damage to my credentials."

"You worry too much."

Soon enough, Oscar said, "Is there anything that you want to comment on for my paper?"

"Erm, let's see. Don't say that I didn't do it for the money but that I felt that he was mentally unstable when I took him on."

"You think that's news? He passed his psychological analysis report: He was fit for the trail."

"I know that but I was stuck with him after his shocking not-guilty plea!"

Oscar smiled. "I'll make you *prince charming* for taking up the case." He seemed to make a toast with his half-filled glass. "Why not write a book?" he asked.

"And end up just like him? Becoming deranged beyond measure."

"So let me write that book, we could make millions on this. Think about it."

"We could indeed," Sebastian responded and winked at him. "So what do you want to know?"

"What do you think he means that he's *innocent* and *nothing made him do it*?"

Sebastian froze for a moment. "If I remember something on what he said, it has everything to do with working in the Foreign Office. He told me in his exact words: *It is to defeat the dark world.*"

Oscar was bemused. "A ghost of some sort, right?"

"That's what it seems he was trying to tell me but I told him not to deviate from the facts. He should have pleaded that he's guilty and the Judge would have considered a lesser sentence."

"But he still claimed to be innocent."

"We had agreed that he was guilty before he changed his story. He's a fucking nut-case."

"Sebastian, just don't worry about your reputation as a lawyer. I will reveal your true nature to my editor. We'll run our story that he'd changed his plea and that he should have been locked up in a mental institution."

"Thanks pal," he said and patted him on his shoulder.

Oscar asked, "You do remember the good old days?"

"What? When you were in the army?"

"We were both in the army, but you left because you broke that ankle of yours during basic training."

"Well, at least I've managed to find a better job."

"So it may seem, friend," Oscar continued, "but I've managed to enrol with the SAS."

"So you did. Then again, you left to take up journalism."

He nodded. "I just wanted time out. Most people in the SAS leave the life: It's very demanding."

"Just who would've taken you on as a journalist? It's not that you're using your survival skills to report behind enemy-lines."

"You could be right. Anyway, many ex-SAS men leave to start their own security firms."

Sebastian added, "You left to take up journalism. You write information for Londoners to comprehend that a madman had a terrifying grudge of not getting published."

Oscar responded, "So you say." He began his reverie. "Sometimes I do miss the life. I miss having those adventures in the Cambodia jungles."

"So why don't you join the SAS again? I mean you're sick of being a civvy. You're always keeping yourself fit and you'll be readmitted — easy peasy."

"I could," he nodded. "I could indeed be reassigned into the SAS. I just miss those adventures. I only left because I felt Captain Blackwater was trying to squeeze me out. Constant PT and PT that. It was every day. I just needed out."

"So why didn't you just join the regular army than—"

"Don't you want me to help you regain the confidence of your local clients, or what?"

Sebastian jokingly said, "Don't get too hasty on how you'll exonerate me."

Clive smiled and drank his last gulp. "You do ask a lot from me since I'm the journalist. It's in my nature, not yours."

The pub was getting livelier as a jukebox started playing a Madonna track: *Like a Virgin*. Oscar looked behind to see who was playing it and saw an old man walking away towards the bar counter. He doesn't know him — but was profiling as that was what the SAS had taught him on recognising potential targets! (Oscar thought that the man was rejoicing his days as a young man; something that made him appreciate life)

"Oi!"

Oscar turned to his front—

"So you like Madonna, don't you?" Sebastian asked.

"She's a fine singer."

"You wanna take him home, don't you?" He pointed at the old man sitting at the counter.

"You've gone soft!" Oscar laughed.

"OK pal," Sebastian said, "make me look pretty for the cameras."

He shook his head. "Hardly necessary as nobody knows who you were defending. In a million years, nobody is going to remember you with that lunatic."

"That doesn't stop rivalry to steal my high-profile clients that I'm only a money-grabber. That isn't bullshit, you know that."

"How many times do you need to mention that?"

"As long as it takes, to drill into your thick skull of yours, I don't want to been known that I'm a money-grabber."

"I better get heading back to my office. My editor would kill me if I don't return within the next 30 minutes."

"That's a poor excuse. Why not call him and say where you are?"

"Are you mad? I must get this story up and running for tomorrow's print."

CHAPTER 2

OSCAR TOOK THE elevator to the fourth floor. As the doors swung open, he made his way to his cubicle—

"Stuart wants to see you in his office."

Oscar knew his colleague sitting at a work station nearby. He smiled after approaching her. "What have I done now?"

"He wants to see you," she said seriously.

He tried to put on a straight face but failed by his grin. Anyway, the joker headed towards the male toilets. Oscar looked straight into the mirror to see if he was presentable. He pulled out his mouth spray too. Looked again and hoped that he wasn't in the firing-line. Afterwards, he made his way to the elevator for the sixth floor.

***

"Where have you been? We do work at God's speed for our readers. You do know that, don't you?"

Oscar attempted to show his remorse. "Stuart," he said, "I'm very sorry for not getting here a lot sooner. I was in that gallery when every fucking reporter was pushing around me to leave."

"Take a seat," his boss said.

Stuart's office was very spacious than any other working-space in the building. One of his walls had hung pictures of him being at special events: Lord Mayor's dinner; attending the London Marathon; shaking hands with Prince Charles at a theatre. Basically, it was all about him being a very-important-person in the heart of London. He loved the city more than perhaps anybody else did — it was rumoured that he fired an employee for supporting a football team outside of the city. His front desk was adjoined to another at the corner. So forth, Stuart was surrounded on three sides: the front; the one on his left and the other behind. The rear wall had his prized pictures and fitted cupboards above them. The left desk had his computer terminal and telephone. The floor was carpeted and it was the only place with it. To Stuart's right, there was a leather concave sofa around a coffee table too, and only his chairman and the board had the right to take a seat there. Also, to the reporters, it was known as the *dreaded sofa,* and it was where Stuart would sit you if he felt that your resourcefulness was in question. There was an office chair, opposite Stuart's front desk, which Oscar gladly claimed. A lot of light was present as the exterior walls were made of glass. In fact, the building was named the *Glass House.*

"You wanted to see me, sir."

"Of course I do want to see you. Explain what you have been doing for the last two hours?"

"I've spoken to Clive Roberts' lawyer."

Stuart reacted, "It takes two hours to speak a lot of bull crap that Clive Roberts is as guilty as Jack the Ripper?" He was shaking his head before looking at his pictures on the wall. "So what did he say?"

"As we already know, he thinks that his client is a madman."

Stuart giggled. "So you wasted two hours of our time to just walk into my office that your source thinks he's mad?"

Oscar had better come up with something great. He cleared his throat. "I sat with him because I wanted to know what changed him. According to my source, Clive Roberts has strong feelings about Europe."

"So what did he say?"

"When he was representing him," Oscar conjectured, "he claims that he wanted to *defeat the dark world*. Also, it's rumoured that his madness began in Greece. Of course, it's just before he handed in his resignation."

"So you're telling me that it took two hours to—"

"Stuart, please," he intervened, "it was hard enough trying to meet up with the Barrister."

The editor was tapping on his desk with his Parker pen. "Hmm, I want your report on my desk within the hour."

Oscar got up and left for the fourth floor.

***

"So you aren't fired, today."

"Lucy, I'm a little tied up. I'll be with you soon," Oscar responded as he got closer to his area.

His computer was already on and entered in his password. He had prepared a draft about Clive Roberts — it was obvious that he was guilty! All he had to do was confirm the Judge's sentence. Also, he thought to dabble on his *dark world* as well. He wrote that the man was suffering acute schizophrenia, and the actual report was done within ten minutes. He smiled on how good he was at getting the article done on time and swirled in his chair as if precocious. He then decided to see Lucy.

"So what are you up to?"

Lucy turned to face him briefly. She hated his attitude by his constant behaviour of somehow being elusive on being sacked. She was a hard-worker too. "I'm writing about the former Lord Mayor's defeat."

"I would like to take you out some time. So how about having a drink with me, after work?"

She answered softly, "Impossible."

Impossible? Oscar thought since he knew that she detested him. But could there be a chance that she was slightly fond of him? "Impossible, why?" he asked.

"I'm writing this report for one."

"I mean straight after, Lucy. I just had an awful day chasing a barrister for information, and I have to write my news correspondence within the next forty minutes."

Lucy stopped typing and was staring at him. "Why aren't you finishing that report? He'll let you go."

Oscar shook his head before he started to admit. "I did most of the work yesterday. Don't you see? I was chasing anybody who knew that mad man."

Lucy smiled. "Alright," she said, "just one drink, OK?"

"Do you finish in forty minutes?"

"We go when you're ready."

Oscar thoughts went wild on what might the night hold? He returned to his computer and sent his final draft to the editor by email. It had the headline: DEFEAT THE DARK WORLD. Soon enough, his phone rang.

"Yes, it's Oscar Brooks."

"Get your arse back up here!"

***

His editor nodded to his report. "This might make it onto the front page."

"You like it sir?"

"It's just what Londoners need to read."

"Is that why you got me in here?"

"Of course it is! Now you listen to me very carefully. I said that your article might make it onto the front page, didn't I?" Oscar nodded enthusiastically. "But," Stuart continued, "I cannot allow it onto the front page."

"I don't understand why you're thinking that Londoners deserve a good read but they aren't permitted to? I mean, I was chasing a barrister this afternoon on his intake; it'll be the most talked of in our time. I cannot think of anything being so close to this, isn't it? Stuart, you'll be making a mistake for our readers."

"It's that barrister that you've mentioned in your article. You may have been chasing him around the court room to say *hello* but he has to go."

"It's what will make our paper stand out against the rest. We are the only paper that knows that the Barrister and that murderer had agreed to a guilty plea. There wasn't really a dark world until Clive Roberts decided to make that one up. He was trying to fool the jury that he was schizophrenic: He's a cold and calculated murderer, you do see that?"

"We let our London readers decide that, not you," he replied. "Personally, I'd agree with you but we aren't competing to be a national paper. All that we're required to do is make news that affects London alone. Once we start moving away from that path, we'll be competing with the big guns. It isn't practical since our shareholders will be expecting a lot more from us. Don't you understand?"

"So why aren't they chasing the Barrister around the court room?" Oscar asked sarcastically, "What if our paper actually knows the identity of Jack the Ripper, do we let that revelation just slip-by because of the big papers?"

The editor got up from his seat and asked his employee to join him along the *dreaded sofa*. Oscar had never sat there before — he now knew that he was going to get an earful.

"We must make our news clean and relevant for Londoners. We are not going to sell papers in Glasgow, Belfast or even in New York. If we were then I will be glad to add the views of a barrister. If I follow your lead today, we'll gain a lot of attention from big investors. If those people start showing interest in us, they'll be expecting something in return. Therefore, I would need to always impress readers in New York, Glasgow, Belfast etc."

"What's the harm in having a big story than anyone else from time-to-time?"

"Investors! Haven't you been listening?"

"So if those *big guns* neglected a story, we must take cover because we'll get too big, right?"

"The moment my Chairman wishes to be bigger; I'll be glad to take up your complete edition. But at the moment, I cannot allow the view of that barrister on the front page."

"But it's true. He recommended on telling the truth: He lied on his plea."

"It's better that it's omitted. We are running a story about Clive Roberts not his care worker."

Oscar was perturbed a little. "Care worker?"

"Your friend took up the case because he felt some kind of bizarre pity for him; a man that wanted his diary published but his victims wouldn't allow it. It's a simple comprehension that Clive was covetous. Other words, his victims had the print-wheel and he didn't."

"But the barrister with Clive had already agreed on the guilty plea."

"We are only a local paper and what's the point about putting that on the front page? No leave it out."

"I've told the barr—"

"Do you wish to carry on working for me? I just gave you a glimpse into the business world of our paper. For heaven's sake, I've been waiting for you for the last three hours for this article. And your excuse is that you were chasing that barrister around Old Bailey. And the fact that he's stupid enough to tell you about that original plea says it all! I don't want that running on my front page, do you understand now?"

Oscar simpered. "I'm sorry, you're absolutely right."

"Good sport. I fancy what you've already written. Also, I do like that headline: DEFEAT THE DARK WORLD. That's absolutely fine."

"Thanks Stuart."

"That antique letter opener that you have?"

"Yes. What of it?"

"Don't you want to sell it on to me? If I remember correctly, that was the reason why I took you on."

Oscar smirked. "If I sold you that then you'll get rid of me a lot sooner, isn't it?"

Stuart laughed too. "So may I borrow it for a short time?"

"Why?"

"I just want to share it with my friends that it was made in Victorian London," Stuart said fondly.

"Why not."

***

Oscar was waiting for service and feeling terrible. He promised Sebastian of being *exonerated* by his paper but he was a liar.

"And what are you having, sir?"

"A pint of Newcastle Brown and a glass of white wine, please."

The bar maid was swift on his orders and Oscar carried them to a table where Lucy was sitting. She was beautiful and had short ginger hair and had a toned body. Since Oscar worked at the London Eagle, summer made her look a stunner: short skirt; high heels and those pretty blue eyes — he wanted her badly and she knew it.

"Congratulations for being on the front page."

"It's nothing," Oscar responded.

"Aren't you happy about it?"

"Of course, yes. But—"

She giggled. "You seem so sweet saying that!"

Oscar wasn't sure what was her body language? *Does she want me this evening? I'm on the front page…Yes! She wants to be a winner!* He thought to himself—

"Lucy, it'll be great to see my name all over London. It was hard work chasing a barrister for information. Also, I tried to get hold of the Judge."

Lucy seemed intrigued. "The Judge! How?"

Oscar took a swig of his Brown. "I basically asked that barrister to give me a mention."

Lucy didn't detect his lie and wanted more. She placed her elbows onto the table and held her head by her hands. Also, she was looking deep into his eyes. "You're amazing when you want to be."

"Lucy, will you stay for another drink?"

"Why ask? I haven't finished drinking my first?"

"OK. Perhaps it's to do with work. God, fucking Stuart!"

Lucy crossed her arms and was sitting up straight. "What the hell has Stuart got to do with covering the story?"

"Nothing, just that I wanted to run something special on our paper but Stuart thinks that it'll give us too much attention from bad investors."

"So what was it?"

"Clive Roberts originally agreed with the Barrister that he was guilty."

"That wouldn't matter. He told the police that he wasn't guilty."

"He was charged. He didn't admit to anything."

Lucy looked embarrassed. "Oops. So I got mixed-up with his actual plea in his trial."

Oscar heard his phone vibrating in his pocket. He looked to see who it was: Sebastian. He couldn't tell him what just happened and so turned off his phone.

"Who was that, your girlfriend?"

"I don't have a girlfriend. It's just a friend I was supposed to help out a little."

Lucy finished her glass and grinned at him. "Details, please?"

"You know that special thing I wanted to add onto my article about Clive Robert's barrister?" She was slightly perplexed but nodded before he went on. "He was worried about losing clients who may see him as a maniac for representing him. He does have several big foreign clients based here in London."

Lucy laughed. "So that's why you turned up late because the pair of you was catching up on old times. So you made a lousy excuse to Stuart that you've found a big story."

Oscar tried to shake his head but smiled. "You're right, Lucy."

"And if Stuart was to hear about this, he would fire you, wouldn't he?"

"Right again, Lucy. So may I buy you another drink?"

She shook her head.

"Come on, you've got me against the wall. I'm your humble servant."

"So answer your friend!"

Oscar pulled an ugly face and took out his phone. He proceeded to turn it on to call him.

"Hiya, it's me Oscar."

"Is everything good?" Sebastian asked him.

"Listen pal. It's not going to happen. My editor won't put you on the front page."

"Why the fuck not?"

"It's not the interest for Hammersmith and Chelsea—"

"My clients have offices in London so they don't have the right to know the score?"

Oscar looked at Lucy. She was teasing him with her empty glass of wine at hand. He turned his attention onto Sebastian. "This might sound shitty but I sat with the editor in his business suite; it's his special place on how our paper sees itself in the years to come. He feels that your name mentioned will attract the wrong type of people into the business: It's too exclusive that nobody else has."

"We sat in the pub together about this. You were all fucking high and mighty that I'll be given a voice. In case you haven't fucking notice, wanker, you're making it a lot more difficult for my clientele to stay with me. Companies like French nuclear energy, bankers etc. That's a loss well over thousands of pounds. You owe me."

"I hear ya, Sebastian. But my editor is a tight arse—"

Oscar looked straight onto Lucy. "He hung up."

"I'm not surprised. It looks like you lost a good friend and good friends are hard to come by."

"So you want another drink? I'm buying."

She wondered, "Do I want another drink? Are you sure you want to have another one after losing a good friend?"

"I need one—"

Lucy rose up. "No you don't, Oscar. Let's leave here together."

CHAPTER 3

OSCAR'S LEGS FELT heavy as he tried to move them forward. He wasn't physically going anywhere as he dropped his running pace. Out of breath, he could feel his body wanting him to give up his goal but he wouldn't. What he was taught in the SAS was that it was the mind that was going to outsmart the body. He pushed forward as hard as he could, harder still to complete his objective.

He had conquered his fate. He could now remove himself from the treadmill and take a seat on the bench close by. Oscar felt his legs weighing a ton and he spread them out in front of him. He wanted to do more; work on his arms. Oscar thought for a long time to head towards another machine. Nowadays, he wasn't as fit being out of the army because he was drinking a lot more. Also, he hadn't been visiting the gym for a long while.

"Are you OK?"

Oscar looked up at the stranger. "I'm good thanks. I'm just getting too lazy that's all."

"You've been on that treadmill for over two hours without a break. You should call it a—"

"Don't worry about me. I used to be in the armed forces. Physical training and more PT was our motto."

The Gym Instructor was staring at him. "I was in the Parachute Regiment and nobody would dream to do that intense workout. What regiment were you in?"

Oscar giggled. He knew that being in the SAS, nobody should reveal their past as a civilian. To make such a revelation would make him a target for IS, IRA or even a similar terrorist group. "Would you believe that I was in the Special Forces," he replied.

"What like the Royal Marines?"

"Something like that," Oscar answered.

"Just take it easy. I know that army life can get tough on physical training. God, I remember vividly an old man in the SAS but died from a cardiac arrest."

Oscar tried to imagine who could have been his friend — the SAS was a relatively small unit and everybody knew one another. "Who was he?" he asked.

"I'm talking years past. My father."

Oscar felt a little uncomfortable and started to sit up straight. "I'm sorry to hear about your old man."

"I was just a child then and that's now history," he added.

By that time, Oscar's legs seemed to be game and he rose up. "I do understand where you're coming from. So why did you leave the Paras?"

He responded again, "I was just going to ask you the same. I left to start up this gym." He raised a hand and pointed at all of his equipment.

"That's quite impressive. I left to become a journalist."

The owner burst out laughing. "What you left," he said in a fit, "the life of the Royal Marines to give us news?"

Oscar nodded. "OK, I didn't get on with Colonel Diapers. He was a tight arse. "

"We get tight arses everywhere. What makes you so special?"

Oscar paused in thought: *What makes me so special?* "At the time, it seemed the right thing to do. I was in Afghanistan and after we got pulled out, I needed a break. I saw so much action there that I thought *fuck it I'm gone.* Now I'm just a regular civvy that likes pumping iron."

"Now I understand," the Instructor said. "War can break a man, and it takes guts to admit that. So where did you tour?"

Oscar thought for a moment again: *Do I just tell him that I was in black-ops with the SEALS in finding Osama Bin Laden?* "Well," he finally said, "the area near Pakistan."

"That's pretty blurry. Doing what?"

"My regiment was assigned to track the possible sightings of dangerous Taliban leaders."

The man crossed his arms and nodded as a sign of respect. "Damn something!"

"Anyhow," Oscar added, "I do miss going around the world to enhance our training abilities."

"Like the arctic?"

"Like in the jungles."

"So before going to Afghanistan, you teamed up with the French Foreign Legion. There are supposed to be the king of the jungle, isn't it?"

"Maybe so, but it wasn't our lot."

The owner hummed before saying. "So what type of news do you do?"

"I've done the story on Clive Roberts."

"That psychopath! But that was over a week ago. So what news are you doing now?"

"Well, I'm just done the report on the Lord Mayor's Parade."

He looked less interested in him. "Aye," he said, "Well it's been nice talking to ya. The name's Josh."

They both said their farewells before Oscar made his way onto a different machine.

Before taking his position to work on his arms, he thought that he better try to speak to Sebastian — they hadn't spoken to each other since Lucy encouraged him to. Beforehand, they used to go out drinking at bars and going to clubs together. Speaking of clubs, if the pair left the night without a girl at hand, they would head straight to Soho. The place had changed from being a renowned spot to find sex to restaurants. It was the latter that they enjoyed! Of course, he was supposed to keep up with his bargain that he was going to praise

Sebastian. He headed to the males locker room to retrieve his phone.

"Sebastian, it's me Oscar."

"Just what the hell do you want?"

"Can we still be friends?"

"After that frigging promise? Have you lost ya tiny mind? I've already lost three big clients."

"Sebastian, please." Oscar had the spirit of the moment, something in his mind wanted to get out. "I mean, what the fuck were you doing representing Clive Roberts in the first place?"

"Oh my God, you've really lost ye tiny mind, haven't you? Don't you remember our night out in Bakersfield?"

"Oh yeah," Oscar conceded, "I really did say that you should go to Luxembourg to defend Clive."

"And so I did. Besides, all you had to do was mention that that freak changed his guilty plea," Sebastian said.

"Look, I'm really sorry. I will make it up to you, and that's a promise."

"So how ya gonna do that? Become the new editor of the London Eagle?"

"Look, the paper is covering some shitty stories recently and we will be taking a hit if our sales don't improve sharpish." Oscar paused after he heard him humming. "I will be able to make it an exclusive story about that plea."

"Oh you fucking wish!"

"So can we continue to be the best of mates?"

"We'll see."

Sebastian ended the call before he gave Oscar the chance to say goodbye.

He shrugged his shoulders and dialled a different number.

"Hiya, it's me Oscar."

"What do you want?" Lucy said alarmed.

"What I want is to inform you that since you made that recommendation to speak to my best friend, he's blanking me."

"It was your call, not mine."

"Now I haven't got him as a friend."

Lucy asked angrily, "What the hell do you want from me?"

"I'm sorry," Oscar replied, "he just hung up on me and I just had to—"

"Text him. Say how you'll get this shit straightened out."

"Thanks, why couldn't I've thought of that?"

"Because you've lost your tiny mind!" Lucy answered jokingly.

"So what are you doing now, Lucy?"

"I'm going out with my boyfriend. Get a life, Oscar," she responded and hung up too.

This is the life, he thought after the call ended abruptly. Oscar placed his phone in his sports bag and went to a vending machine to purchase a still drink. From there, he imagined being too boring for anyone's company: He hadn't many friends. *No matter,* he thought as he proceeded to go towards a workout machine, *I'm gonna work on these muscles*.

***

After freshening-up in the changing rooms, he made his exit out of the building. He took in the fresh air and the immediate sights of London that evening. It wasn't a popular place for tourists but it was a great area to live.

So many things to do and he was a fanatic Fulham supporter. He felt his phone vibrating in his pocket. He reached in to read the message from Sebastian...No wait, it was a text sent directly from a stranger:

u need to tell the world about this.

u will be making history

He texted back:

Do you have a story that u wish 2 share?

As soon as that was sent, he got another:

Yes, I trust you.

Can U C me at the Plush café

Oscar felt settled on why somebody wanted to meet him there. It was his local place to eat his breakfast before going to work, and was wondering if it had anything to do with the café assistant. Speaking of which, he had longed to take her out but she was just as difficult as Lucy.

He received another text:

Can U meet me in1 hr?

Oscar replied that he was able to get there within ten minutes and started to cross the road. He buttoned up his jacket after he felt the chill across his neck. He also leapt over a huge puddle along the pavement. He saw a mother with her infant daughter looking at it and cursed the local council for not sorting out her borough — she went around it. Oscar carried on moving towards the Plush Café which was just around the corner onto Queen's Lynn. He entered and took a seat facing the window outside.

A man approached him and produced a huge smile. "Well, Mister Reporter, what can I do to honour this occasion?"

"Tea please."

"Milk too?"

He nodded and started to look outside at the London Eagle building. One might argue that it belonged in the financial district due to its design. It had six floors. The fourth floor — where he worked — had thirty members of staff. There were eighty employees ranging from cleaners to the editor too. The paper generated its money through advertising and it gave free home delivery service for the London boroughs as well.

"I do recognise you."

Oscar turned away from the picturesque outside and saw a young woman standing in front of him.

"Can we move away from this window?" she asked.

Oscar acknowledged her and they took their seats at the rear of the café. Also, he received his cup of tea there. "Do you wish to have a cup of tea?"

"No."

He also recognised her as the woman crying alone in the gallery. She was very attractive to be in company of. "So then," Oscar said being professional, "how may I help you?"

"I remember you in the gallery," she said

"We met at the gallery?" Oscar replied awkwardly. "Ah yes! The trial of Clive Roberts so how may I help you?"

"He's my father."

Oscar's conjecture was right so it wasn't much of a surprise at all. As far as he could tell, she was going to tell him that she was ashamed of him or not. *Oh boy*, he thought, *why did I put myself into this position?* Then he imagined having a fabulous evening with her.

"You wrote in your report the words: DEFEAT THE DARK WORLD. What did you mean by that?"

He wooed. "Mad'am, madness goes where it pleases. It can be unforeseen out there; out of our sights and minds," he magnanimously answered.

"Do you believe in what you are saying?"

Oscar nodded passionately. "Of course, I meant every word of it, and the source using that phase was your father. He'd surely given it to us to seek answers."

"If you really meant it, then you're a danger."

Oscar choked on his tea. Of course, he was trying to beguile her to bed. After she mentioned that he was in a peril state, he hadn't the interest. "What are you talking about woman?"

"Look, just having me here might have been a mistake. My dad was trying to expose the dark world. You do seem the type that wants to make that revelation, don't you?"

He looked bemused by her explanation. "My paper isn't in the business to believe in conspiracy theories. If you felt that my article justified it, I could lose my job for leaving subliminal messages in the report."

She looked confused. "What are you talking about?"

Oscar hadn't a clue so didn't respond.

"All that I'm saying is that if you want to dig for the truth, you will very soon." She handed him her contact details on a piece of folded paper. "Trust me," she continued, "you will soon learn why."

She was about to leave but Oscar held her back. "Is this some kind of a practical joke?"

"Trust me, Oscar."

CHAPTER 4

IT WAS EASY enough placing one foot in front of the other. Except that Oscar nearly tripped over a step as he stretched outside. He longed for Lucy that evening and she knew he had the hots for him — yet they hadn't the right chemistry since Lucy was fairly sober. She was asked if she loved him and he was placing his hands on her hips. For her, it wasn't a romantic proposal; it was torture. Besides, she was accompanied by her new boyfriend — oddly enough a barrister — at the pub. After Lucy informed her new partner that Oscar served in Afghanistan, the already troubled man wanted to pick a fight with him. There was a brief indignation but Lucy took him home. Oscar didn't want to ponder on what it meant for her to take him home so drank his usual pint. In fact, he drank eight pints before the last order call. Of course, Oscar staggered out of the pub and was reading the time on his watch: 11.35pm. He was at peace standing still; he had been breathing heavily inside and the freshness was compelling.

"You're the man!"

He turned to face the pub entrance and saw a jovial stranger wanting to shake his hand. "I was just drinking my ale," he replied, shaking his hand too.

"Yeah right," he said sarcastically, "Lucy was all over you!"

Oscar could only smile. "Good night," he responded.

The man went on his merry way and Oscar still stood there inhaling the cool breeze into his lungs. *Now let's get home,* he thought. In his mind, it was easily said than done as his body was making him walk in a zigzag fashion. He looked around himself feeling obscure on his whereabouts; he saw shutters upon a premise. After he cursed himself for not having a clear perception of the shop after it closed, he found his dimly lit alley which was the short cut home.

"Excuse me, sir."

Oscar heard a posh accent behind him and thought straight away that the stranger was lost. He turned around and produced a very friendly smile — dare I say exaggerated — to the gentleman who was accompanied by another man. "How may I help you?"

"Is that the way to the Good Mews apartments?"

Oscar nodded and pointed into his direction. "It's just over there. Are you lost?"

"Funny of you to ask," he replied. "I don't think I am."

Oscar was thinking that the two strangers were very peculiar. *They're far too well-dressed and are probably punters looking for sex,* he thought quietly.

"Sir, may I trouble you once more?"

Oscar responded, "Look I am very drunk so you have to excuse—"

"Come on, just one more favour and that's all that I'll ask?"

"What do you want?"

"Do you have a phone that I may borrow?"

"What do you want with my phone as there's a payphone straight ahead in the car park, okay?"

"You see," he said, "I just want your phone."

Oscar felt an ebullition coming on as he spoke to them. "No I don't have one but I'll see you later." He moved on quickly but could hear the soles of their shoes picking up quicker. He turned again. "Look hear!" he shouted, "leave me in peace!"

"You do need to calm down," the man said and produced a hand gun from his coat pocket. "Give me your phone."

Strange, he thought, *they don't look like typical thieves.* "OK, you can have my phone," he acknowledged.

"That's very good indeed," he said. "I recognise you being a reporter from the London Eagle, isn't it?"

"Yeah that's right."

"Can you explain why you're passionate about *defeating the dark world?*"

"It's just that—" Oscar recalled what Sebastian told him. "What do you want from me?"

The man laughed. "I already told you: Your phone."

"Can I leave now?"

"Of course you can. However, I haven't introduced you to my dearest friend, Max."

"This is just too easy," Max said and got closer to Oscar. "I'm going to make a threat that you never saw us. Do you understand?"

Oscar was bemused about it all. "You're stealing my phone and you think that you can prevent me from reporting this to the police?"

Max laughed. "I wasn't thinking straight was I?" His right hand rolled into a ball and he pulled his arm back. He followed it though across Oscar's face. After watching him fell, he carried on hitting him on his head but Oscar was defending himself with his arms. Max began kicking him hard elsewhere to break his protection and was finding ways to punch him some more. "I'm mugging you isn't it you arsehole!"

"Enough," the man holding the gun said, "let's leave that faggot."

"Oh and one more thing," Max said to Oscar, "you better take care of yourself because you might end up being defeated by the dark world."

Oscar felt his ribcage tightening. He placed his hand on his forehead and saw that he was bleeding a bit. *Who were they and what did they really want?* He tried to pick himself from the floor. In pain, he wondered if he should visit his local hospital but carried on heading home.

***

He opened his front door and made his way into the bathroom. One of his eyes was swollen and his left cheek too from the punches. His phone was stolen with all his contacts on it as well. "That fucking wanker, if I had it my own way I would've done them proper!" he managed to say.

Oddly enough, he remembered that woman giving him her number in the café. He also recalled her saying that *he will soon learn why?* Oscar wasn't sure what he was getting himself involved into but felt that he had better contact her discreetly. Anyhow, he washed his face and put on a plaster across his eyebrow. Next was to take a seat on his sofa to watch a bit a telly. Luckily, he didn't have to go to work the following morning and so passed out.

CHAPTER 5

"YOU LOOK TERRIBLE," Lucy said as Oscar walked passed her.

"I got mugged three nights ago: My phone," he replied as he took his place.

Lucy got up from her seat and moved towards his space. "Have you reported it to the police?"

"Of course," he responded.

"Look at the state of you; you shouldn't be here working today. Haven't you mentioned this to Stuart?"

"No. But I will."

"Tell him now," Lucy said, "or I will tell him."

Oscar got up and still felt his chest tightening as he made his way. Everybody on the floor could see that he was hurt — they all knew that he served in the army in Afghanistan, and it seemed uncanny that to return home was more dangerous. Obviously, his colleagues were muttering amongst themselves on their observation. Nearly everybody, on the entire floor, was at the pub three nights ago too. It didn't bother him what they thought as he tried to pass by them.

"Got yourself into a fight?"

"I got mugged," Oscar informed as he entered into the elevator.

"I hate crime waves and that's especially since we all live in London."

"I hate them too," Oscar agreed before the elevator doors closed.

He pressed for the editor's floor, waited patiently and the doors swung open. The journalist saw some people staring at him as he made his way to his office; the members of staff working on that floor were human resources and finance. Oscar was vehement to get to his destination and knocked on his door. He got his permission to enter and turned the door knob.

"So what in the world has been happening to you?" Stuart asked when he saw him approaching his desk.

"I was mugged several nights ago."

Stuart sat there staring at him as he was trying to believe on what he heard. "So what did they take?"

"My phone."

"I know London is known to have dark alleys and this is terrible. So where were you walking?"

"I was walking home from the local pub," Oscar responded.

Stuart was stupefied. "Haven't you seen a doctor?"

"No I haven't."

"You cannot turn up to work looking like shit without medical attention. You of all people should have known that."

"Well, I do feel—"

"You don't seem fit to work."

"Should I take a couple days off?"

"That's if you do seek medical attention. I want you to see your doctor and then report back here in a couple of days," Stuart said.

Oscar never knew the soft side of his boss. He was always demanding from people to not under-perform, but to get beaten up he seemed a fairly nice person. "I will go now."

"Looks like I will need to sort you out a new mobile and a new set of business cards. Go now. Leave!"

Oscar exited his office. He walked a little and immediately thought about the woman giving him her card in the café. She had warned that danger would pursue him just by believing in the term: *DEFEAT THE DARK WORLD.* Some people were staring at him as he stood there thinking; they also looked away after he returned their glances.

.

***

Leo held his breath as he raised his legs to swing upon his cushion seat. The pain was sudden but past; he sighed in relief. Oscar obtained another cushion and started to puff it up and rested his head on it. It was strange for him to being idle as he appreciated his room that he furnished for the first time ever. The clock was stating that it was three in the afternoon and below that was his television — switched off. In the living room, he could see the bottom frame of his huge mirror hanging above the sofa. He wanted to see the state that he was in but couldn't pose correctly.

"Those bastards," he said cursing. "Just who the hell do they think they are?" he now whispered to himself.

Oscar admired his tea lights; three were lit which produced a mint scent on the coffee table close by. The room was creamy white — like the rest of his apartment

— which had several sculptures positioned at a corner. At the opposite end by his television and clock; there stood his cabinet with a telephone on it. So there he was thinking to call that woman. But wasn't it absurd? That she thought that he would face peril. Anyhow, he was a journalist and in his profession, he ought to investigate to make news. Steadily he got up before searching into his cabinet where he kept coupons, vouchers and utility bills. He dashed it in there but was annoyed with himself on being careless. Eventually, he found that number. Oscar sat next to his telephone and it only rang just for a few moments.

"This is Oscar is…" he said and was hesitating to read her name. "Is that Amanda?"

"Yes, and who are you?"

"Don't you remember that we met at the café?"

"Oh it's the journalist from the London Eagle, isn't it?"

"Aye. Look can we talk?"

"Have you lost your phone?"

Oscar was surprised by her response. "What kind of game are you playing?"

"If you really believe DEFEAT THE DARK WORLD, what were you expecting?"

"Well. Not to get robbed for my phone by armed thugs is my probable answer."

"So you were using me?"

"Amanda, I hardly know you. I'm a journalist for Christ sake!"

"So be on your guard."

"Look I don't want to chat over the phone," Oscar said. "Can we meet up somewhere quiet?"

"Sure."

***

Some of the children were running impatiently to see things whilst others enjoyed their immediate sighting. It stood there looking at his admirers but wandered off to gain attention elsewhere. The youngsters were amazed at the size of it as it departed.

"Mr. Harrison," one of them shouted at the top of her voice, "where is it going?"

"Don't worry," he replied, "it's only going for a walk."

It was a blessing, everybody cherished the breeze and the shade since it was hot. Amanda was observing the elephants in their habitat at the London Zoo. The trees around her were rustling and it was delightful to take refuge. She could see an ice cream van parked a distance away and the thought of a special treat seemed too good to have but she wouldn't. Amanda wasn't there to enjoy herself since she was there to meet up with Oscar. She had considered that the zoo would have been quiet during the weekdays that afternoon. Many times she shook her head in disbelief as she saw scores of infants passing through. She was expecting to meet him by the bush which was shaped like an elephant...He was five minutes late. His lateness had given her time to think on why she got Oscar involved? Her answer was that there wasn't anybody giving her any hope: To conquer the dark world. She was well aware of the dangers to take the gauntlet from her father, and Oscar did seem very brave. But still, there wasn't any sign of him. She took out her phone to ring him...No answer. Amanda felt fragile and wanted to scream at the top of her voice that he was playing her as a fool. *Why else would Oscar use the phase: DEFEAT THE DARK WORLD?* she thought to herself. The girl stood there in hope as teachers led their pupils from hither to thither. Amanda to stand by the elephant shaped-bush was making her feel that she was the attraction as there were many photos being taken in her direction. How she wanted to move away but her embarrassment would linger — a lot of the visitors there were drawn to her than the bush and the elephants! *Hope,* she thought after seeing him approaching her. Amanda was smiling but faded after seeing him limping. It troubled her for a moment.

"I'm sorry that they hurt you," Amanda said as it became clear of his injuries.

"OK. So what have you got me involved with?"

"All that I can tell you is that my dad warned me that the British establishment is planning something really big. It will affect all of modern society."

Oscar pondered on it. "It will affect what exactly?"

"My dad got involved in something that wants complete control—"

Oscar was laughing loudly. "So you think," he added, "that I'm James Bond. I'm going to save the world, isn't it?"

She objected. "If those bruises on that face," she continued, "didn't convince you than maybe something more harmful will."

"I will tell you this though," he said, "that I used to be a member of the SAS."

She shook her head. "I don't think your combat skills are required. All you have to do is follow the dotted lines. You just have to believe me that Clive

Roberts has been framed for the murders of his dear friends."

"So I'm the last jigsaw piece to your puzzle because I used the phase DEFEAT THE DARK WORLD, isn't it?"

"Why else would I want to meet you? Look if you don't believe in what I have to say, I'll just leave," she said and looked away to find the nearest exit.

Oscar grabbed her by her arm. "Look here missy, I didn't come all this way to make sport of you. I'm a journalist and I want answers that make fucking sense."

She turned to face him. "How dare you take hold of me!"

Oscar was alarmed by her outburst and noticed that everybody around him was watching him. He felt like a monster in front of the children and their teachers after holding her by her shoulders. "How dare I?" he asked. "I'm here for the good—" His cheek, already sore, doubled. He yelped and released her after she found him vulnerable.

Amanda said, "Know your place, boy!"

"Why did you have to hit me so hard?" he said and was trying to ease the pain across his cheek. "I'm sorry. I'm really sorry. Let's find a place to sit so that we can talk a lot more civilised, shan't we?"

"No, let's just walk around the zoo," she insisted.

The pair remained quiet walking passed the elephants section into the chimpanzee area. Of course, the monkeys were enjoying the attention from the visitors smiling and joking with them. Amanda loved monkeys. It was certain as she could be seen clapping lightly when a monkey did a somersault. Oscar wanted to join in but her slap across his cheek was troublesome.

"My father always bought me here after my mother died," she said. "This place brings back some fond memories."

"I know that we haven't come here to admire the chimps. I want to see you about my recent attack."

She was jovial seeing the animals but to hear him moaning changed that. "It may have been a mistake getting you into this shit."

"I told you that I'm a journalist. If there's something you want to tell me, tell me now."

"My father and I were close. He always tells me stuff about working in the Foreign Office." She stopped walking and held onto Oscar's arm. "He wanted to tell me something that the British establishment is up to no good."

Oscar nodded but wasn't sure what she meant. "I'm thinking about Queen and Country. Is that what you're telling me?"

"It's got nothing to do with the Queen. Don't you get it? There's a dark force at work here."

"So if there is such a force, where do I fit in?"

"Why don't you go to Greece because that was where my father had worked?"

Oscar pondered on his editor; Stuart wasn't the type of guy to finance it.

She now asked, "What are you thinking?"

"I could go to Greece," he implied. "I just need to be given the OK from my editor, that's all."

"So you're serious?"

Oscar nodded. "So what do you think I will find in Greece?"

"Anything! Remember, he worked as an Ambassador," Amanda responded.

"Just wait a minute," he said, "you say that danger will pursue me if I get to the truth, right?"

"Oscar, all you have to do is just be careful. Don't run that mouth of yours that the British establishment is up to no good."

"Why do you think it has something to do with Queen and Country?" Oscar asked bemused.

She stormed, "For crying out loud!" Amanda lowered her voice. "Dark force."

"It's a long shot. I just think that there will be dead ends."

Amanda asked, "Look here Oscar, when I anticipated that your phone will be taken I was right, wasn't I?"

"So you say but how did you know?"

"That was exactly what they've done to my father. It's their way to keep track on all of your contacts."

Oscar couldn't think straight. "Are you telling me that I will be framed for some crazy murder?"

"I'm saying that you will need to be careful...A dark force is at play," she replied.

"I feel like I'm going around in circles. Don't you know what it is, the Mafia?"

Amanda wanted to scream at him as she frowned. "What are you talking about?"

"Don't you know what that dark force is?"

"It's not a Sicilian outfit."

"So what is it?"

"And you think that I would have been here asking for your help, don't you?"

"You tell me?" he asked.

"You're a moron!" she said. "I came to you because I was desperate for answers. Yet, all you're doing is expecting I know everything; I do not have all the bloody answers. Do you hear me?"

Oscar made a concession. "I hear you loud and clear." He sighed heavily. "You're hoping that I will find the answers in Greece, isn't it?"

"Just get yourself there and follow the dotted lines."

"You say *dotted lines.* Is that your father's way of saying that there's something in Greece?"

"You tell me?" she asked.

"So why are you helping me?"

"I want to help you to make me understand. We'll be helping each other to understand what we're dealing with."

"So I just go to the Embassy now and I'll find it there. What exactly am I looking for?"

"Trust me," she said, "just go to Greece and you will find what you're looking for."

Oscar admitted, "I'll need to heal up first before making a trip there. Just leave it with me, darling."

CHAPTER 6

IT TURNED OUT that Oscar had a fractured rib and was suffering from internal bleeding after his medical check-up. So it had been a while before Oscar returned to work, and the first floor he attended was the sixth. Everybody appeared to know that he was a victim of a horrific crime. Grinning pass his colleagues, he knocked on the boss' door before entering.

Stuart was busy talking to a journalist when he saw him. He lifted a hand and delineated at him to wait outside. He acknowledged and sat on a chair.

"Are you alright?"

Oscar didn't know him but smiled. "So ya heard about the mugging?"

"Of course, we all heard of it and it's just outright

outrageous. I do hope the police catch those involved," he said before nodding his head. "If you don't mind me asking, what did they look like?"

Oscar replied, "Two white guys dressed-up real slick. I mean that they were wearing suits and rain coats."

"Criminals will do anything to fool us decent folks on our livelihoods."

"What you're saying is absolutely correct."

"I read your article on Clive Roberts," he said. "Outstanding work. So why did you choose the London Eagle?"

"This is my first job in journalism; I used to be a soldier in Afghanistan."

"Were you? Say my name's Duncan and I work on this floor sorting out the payroll."

"It's nice to meet you."

After he gave his farewell, Stuart's office was made available and Oscar was allowed access.

Stuart got up to shake his hand. "It's good to see you again, Oscar. Please take a seat here."

"It's great to back, Stuart."

"I want you to work with Lucy today. You've been away for a full five weeks, and it hurts me to think that you've forgotten how we work."

"That's not a problem."

Stuart got up again to extend a hand. "It's good that you're with us again." After he shook his, he said, "Now scram!"

The editor took a seat behind his desk and yawned loudly. After that, he noticed that Oscar was still standing in front of him. "Is there a problem?"

"If I may be blunt, it's about my front page story on Clive Roberts."

"We already agreed that a barrister's view on the plea wasn't newsworthy, isn't it?" Stuart asked.

"It has nothing to do with that. It's all about Clive Roberts."

Stuart knew that he was trying to encourage him to ask but he was leaning back in his chair; arms folded.

"Stuart," Oscar started to say, "ever since I took up the case about the former Ambassador, I always wanted to dig around on his background."

"You mean that he had a shotgun license and that he fallen out with his ghost-writer and her husband?"

Oscar shook his head. "We know that he resigned his post in Greece because he wanted to publish his diary. It's not that I'm interested in it but why leave a super-duper career?"

Stuart hummed. "It's an interesting point to look into. I could imagine researchers having a field day writing books on that mentally-disturbed character, don't you agree?"

"I would agree with you but this paper should break the news on him," Oscar said.

"We're a small paper with a small budget. I don't see the point to take up that story any further."

"As a reporter, I could visit the embassy and just chat to all of his former staff on what they remembered of him."

Stuart leaned forward in his chair. "If I was to fund such an investigation, why should you take the lead?"

"For one, I have some understanding from his defence lawyer that he had a meltdown in Greece."

Once more, Stuart asked him to take a seat along the *dreaded sofa*. "Oscar, you must understand that our major shareholder—"

"What we must understand is that our major shareholder only wants to make money. Like you said, if we have exclusive news, we'll need to keep on providing such articles that our paper will become a national treasure. Nobody wants to see our shares plummeting, right?"

Stuart really didn't like to see his employee telling him on how to run his paper. He agreed, in partial too, "That's great but you do recall my lesson on this sofa?"

"Just listen to this as this is completely sound: That barrister had a view which is now long passed and our readers will not appreciate any of his old secrets today."

"So why do you want to go to Greece?"

"There is something about Greece that may be an interest for London. I'll go to the country to snoop around and come back with some good shit." Oscar added, "I bring our good shit back here for you to marvel upon. It'll be a worthy investigation because I got a good source that something was going on in Athens. Besides, the trip to Greece won't be much of an expense."

"So who is that source?"

"That gentleman that I mentioned earlier: Sebastian Underwood."

"Oh that barrister, right you are." Stuart said, sounding cautious too. "It seems that you sure know how to use him for the good of London."

"If he wasn't used, I don't think my story wouldn't have been running on the front page."

There was laughter in the room and Stuart asked him back to his desk. "Oscar, you're a diamond geezer! I'll finance the trip!" He was sharpening his pencil when he added. "It will only be you going out there to Greece. However, for the time being I still want you to accompany Lucy now."

***

"Oscar you're back!" Lucy shouted after hugging him. "You do look well."

"Thanks, Lucy. Stuart wants me to work with you today," Oscar said.

"I see."

"What are you snooping on?"

She responded, "I'm looking into our Parish churches, that copper thieves are plundering them."

Oscar thought to himself that her report could have been easily written without seeing the clerics and the police; he felt an excitement about going to Greece where he hadn't a clue what he would stumble upon. In fact, the idea of working with Lucy was just going to be a boring day. "How far are you in this?"

"I've just started now." She continued, "I've got an interview with the reverend tomorrow."

"Do you want me to make calls with the police?"

"Why not," she said and smiled.

***

Oscar exited the police station with Lucy. He felt a droplet on his forehead and looked up into the grey sky. He couldn't tell if it might rain. Nevertheless, they both decided that they were going to a local pub. "It's a bit cloudy today, isn't it?"

"That won't make a difference, will it?"

Oscar got into his red Ford fiesta with Lucy beside him. "It pains me to think that these days, we may need copper traders to become fully licenced."

"That's your opinion. I mean we're dealing with a certain group of sick racketeers."

The driver turned on his ignition to head towards their destination. "I just hope that the police catch those bastards."

Five minutes later, Oscar was looking into his view mirror when he was certain of something occurring. "Isn't that car lost?"

Lucy was looking ahead confused. "Just what the hell are you talking about?"

"I'm talking about the one that's two cars back."

"Oscar, just what are you babbling on about?"

"It may be nothing but we don't usually see a Bentley every day, don't we?"

Lucy turned around and spotted it. She giggled a little too. "Turn left to see what it does."

Oscar was happy to oblige and still the car was trailing behind.

"Now try going right," Lucy now said.

Oscar waited for the incoming traffic to be clear before he made the turn and the Bentley was still behind them close.

"I'll suppose that we can make a turnabout to see what that does," she said.

Oscar agreed, "That's a brilliant idea."

...Lucy just stared at him. "Do you owe some dodgy characters some money?"

"Nah, not me."

"So what does it want?"

"What the hell do I know? I just want to stop at a pub—"

"You ought to take us back to the office, if you don't mind," Lucy insisted.

"I'm sorry about this. I was—"

"Oscar, what are you getting yourself involved into?"

"Okay, it's to do with a woman," he replied.

"So that's her husband?"

"It's hardly her husband. You remember that case, Clive Roberts? Well, he has a daughter who thinks the world of him."

"The rich bastard driving is who?" Lucy pressed on.

"That driver must be part of a circle that the woman is involved in," he said.

Lucy pointed at a random alley. "So is that where you got yourself beaten up?"

"Lucy, please," he added sternly, "you shouldn't make a mockery!"

She apologised.

He said, "When we finish this report, I'm gonna be in Greece."

"Are you going on holiday with that woman?"

"No not on holiday. I'm taking up an investigation on Clive Roberts."

"Oh now I see," Lucy said watching him drive, "that car must be the secret service."

"Why do you say that?"

"Because it seems logical that Clive worked in espionage. So you're getting mixed-up in some sensitive information, aren't you?"

"I haven't a clue on what I'm getting myself into," he admitted.

"So how did you meet that woman?"

"The front cover story that I was doing, she was intrigued."

Lucy pulled a face; cross-eyed and sticking out her tongue. "You do keep odd company!"

"It's true," he insisted.

"So how did you convince Stuart to accept the Greece trip?"

"If you must ask, Stuart isn't aware about the girl (and that car following us). Yet, we did talk that whatever turned Clive into a psychopath, it's everything to do with Athens, not London."

She laughed. "Just being in your company makes me think that I will turn into a mad woman!"

Oscar was getting closer to the London Eagle building and he found a place to park.

Lucy looked around and didn't see the tailing car. "It seems that our paranoia got the better of us today."

***

It took a fortnight to write a series of reports about the copper thieves operating in the Hammersmith area. Also, they were eventually caught and their trials were set in earnest. Oscar found that working with Lucy was a nightmare when she teased him about fancying a beautiful, mysterious and troublesome woman. All of his colleagues, on his floor, knew that he was getting attached to Amanda Roberts. After work, his drinking colleagues would cheer him on about his imminent visit to Greece, and that he scored a new girlfriend! They always shouted: "Three cheers for Oscar getting his way with the girl...And Stuart too!" Of course, it was all due to Lucy's gossiping.

***

"Why in seven bells do I need these?" he asked himself.

He couldn't see it but had a familiar touch. His hand was taking a dip and anticipated a certain lump as he searched; he felt something harder than he expected and pulled it out; his wallet.

"Why did I pack that darn thing in here?" he now asked himself, ashamed too.

He divulged again and his hand appeared to sift through a bundle of feathers. At last he was able to retrieve them; his two wool pullovers. So in their place, he included his sandals before zipping up his rucksack. Oscar proceeded to take the luggage to the front door of his flat and returned to his bedroom. Clothes were everywhere: The floor; on the bed and dressing table. Regardless, he sat on the edge of his bed to rest. It was just as well as Stuart had given him a week to investigate further on Clive Roberts. The idea of going to sunny Greece was compelling, but something was lurking on his mind — *what if I fail?* He had already sat on the dreaded sofa — more than once — and Stuart would be expecting good results. He thumped on his bed hard. Incidentally, his mobile phone began to ring.

"Who is this?"

"So that's how you treat your good and decent friends," Lucy answered.

"I'm sorry. I've got to go to Heathrow this evening. I'm just getting myself set."

"You better find what you're looking for because everybody is going crazy about that woman of yours. Did you know that she's in a national paper claiming that her father is innocent?"

"What!"

"Yeah, she was trying to explain that there's a covert operation that her father was working on."

"Carry on."

"She says that she hasn't a clue what it is," she added. "She'll be destroying your career if Stuart gets to hear that you know her well."

"I told her to keep a low profile while I'll be digging around. Thanks for the heads up," Oscar reacted.

"It's bizarre that you're getting yourself in a right mess. It must be good that you've good friends on our floor, isn't it?"

"I really hope so but the fact is that this assignment is a real game-changer: on becoming the next assistant editor. It cannot go amiss, right?"

She giggled. "As long as we're all bubbly, and you intrigue us all about that woman of yours! Do you really know where to start?"

"The embassy."

"What if that's a dead end?"

"I just got to trust Amanda that I will find something big," he replied.

"I hope so too because if you return with nothing, Stuart will have you."

That's a sweet reminder, Oscar thought to himself. "I really do trust her."

"Not because she's damn pretty?"

"Because I do have two incredible leads," he excused.

"Are the pair of you friends again?"

"We haven't spoken to one another since the front cover," he replied.

Lucy said, "Look here, my boyfriend is asking me into the kitchen. Just be safe, okay?"

Oscar laughed. "Don't worry about me for I was in the army." They ended their call.

He had better return with something from Greece to keep his job. Worse still, Amanda, an attractive woman, had just amplified her persona on being the most talk about woman at his workplace! It just seemed inevitable that Stuart would be letting him go sooner than later for his beguiled approach. He dialled to speak to her.

"Amanda, why did you? Why on earth did you go public?"

"What the hell and who the hell are you to tell me what to do?"

"I've already told you about the delicate situation at work. The editor doesn't know that you're my lead."

"So why don't you tell him?"

"That's because he's a tight arse! If he gets a whiff about us, I lose anything."

"So tell him."

"It's too late now because I had many opportunities to inform him over the last three weeks. He only agreed because he thought our major shareholder would like to hear the development first."

"What are you telling me, you bastard?" Amanda shouted. "Are you telling me that you only got this gig just to amuse your top cronies?"

"Please listen, my boss is a tight arse. I had to charm my way to get the go-ahead. Can you imagine the damage being done when he hears that I was fucking with him?"

Amanda was amused. "Is that why you didn't fancy..." She stopped short. "You're taking this little setback very well. I already told you that once you get to Greece, the answers will be open to you."

"That better be the case or I'll have to find another career."

"Just remember that when you get to the Embassy, use the term: DEFEAT THE DARK WORLD."

"Yeah, right. Also hope that I don't get beaten up by men in rain coats asking for an umbrella!"

She laughed modestly. "Yeah that's right," she added, "and just don't walk down dark alleys, and you'll be just fine."

"I will keep you up-to-date during my stay, Amanda. I only hope you're right."

CHAPTER 7

OSCAR shook his head as he was trying to observe a conveyer belt carrying luggage. While he was trying to be alert, he could hear some people near him relieved as if the worse part of their journey was over. After collecting his, he walked a short distance towards a man in a light blue uniform at a stand. There was also a sign: Nothing to Declare.

"Good evening and welcome to Athens International Airport," he said to Oscar, "may I take a look at your passport?"

Oscar obliged to his request.

"Thank you sir," he said, "you haven't anything to declare?"

He smiled. "No."

"Where's your baggage?"

"I've only bought my rucksack," he answered.

"No suitcase?"

"I always just carry with me a rucksack," he now replied as he turned his back on him to show it.

"You come here all alone on holiday?"

"I'm not a holidaymaker."

The Passport Steward continued to be inquisitive. "I'm sorry, Mr Brooks. But you're here to do what business?"

"Journalism."

"Journalism? But I see only you here? Where is your crew?"

"Freelance Journalism," he excused, "I'm here to find news."

"What kind of news are you seeking?"

"It's about the British embassy in Athens."

"What's wrong with it?"

"The former Ambassador used to work there; he's a convicted murderer."

The Passport Steward asked to look into his rucksack. As he searched through, he said, "Are you sure that you haven't anything to declare?"

"Nothing sir," he replied.

"I see," he said and handed him back his passport and his big luggage. "Please do have a lovely stay."

Oscar couldn't make up his mind where to stop for the week as he left the airport. He made his way outside to flag a taxi.

"Hello there and where may I take you?"

"To the nearest hotel," Oscar responded.

The taxi driver was in a fit of giggles. "You have money?"

"Yes I do, why?"

He still laughed. "Only rich people stop at the nearest hotel. It's full of millionaires and they come to Greece in yachts." The driver said, "You no come in yacht so you visit rich woman?"

Oscar was amused. "Where will you recommend that I go?"

"There is a decent hotel where Britons go. It has a swimming pool, bar and many things. I take you there, yes?"

"Do take me there, thank you," Oscar acknowledged.

***

Oscar paid the driver and retrieved his rucksack. As the taxi moved away, he looked around. He made out some trees swaying in the background and the wind was caressing his face; he heard something sprinkling in the middle of the driveway. Oscar moved closer for he was certain of it a fountain and something loomed above it. It was poorly lit and Oscar considered it a statue — of the hotel founder was what he thought. His eye lids were becoming a little heavy and he hadn't any further interest to inspect it. He could also hear the sound of insects proclaiming the night too. Oscar saw the entrance and proceeded to walk ahead. It had double doors and one was fixed shut while the other wasn't. Still he soldiered on pass them. Brooks emerged into an open space where the floor had a glossy finish. As Oscar took a step forward, he squeaked (which did prevent him from being half asleep). Brooks saw the main desk and continued onwards. Obviously, Oscar got the attention of the receptionist the closer he got. The woman was bemused to see him carrying no suitcases and she tried to smile. Her face dropped when she could hear him still making that noise. Oscar was wearing his new sport shoes and was slightly perturbed. Anyhow, he put on a happy face. "Good evening!"

Before Brooks managed to stand near her, he heard somebody approaching him from behind. Quickly, Oscar turned around and saw a congenial woman. "Hello."

She sounded French but spoke fairly good English. "I haven't seen you here before. Have you arrived here all alone?" She now asked after he nodded, "This is usually a family resort. Are you expecting to see someone tonight?

"No, I just want a room for the week."

"But it's a family resort and you bring no children or wife." She conceded, "However, all guests are welcomed."

"Where do I check in?" Oscar asked clumsy.

"Just continue ahead," she replied and walked away on her own business.

Oscar's shoes were still causing havoc. "Good evening," he said again.

The lady didn't respond but flinched when he got to the counter.

"May I have a room please?"

"Are you here all by yourself?"

"Yes."

"This may not be ideal place to stay because we don't have any spare rooms. I'm very sorry," she said.

"But I've—"

"We do have a two-bedroom suite, if that is of any help?"

Oscar nodded. "I take it please."

"How many nights are you planning to stay?"

"Six."

"Are you paying by credit card?"

"Yes, so how much will that be?"

She was processing the details before coming up with the sum. "That's €1700."

Oscar was thinking that the taxi driver had in fact taken him to the next expensive place to stay over. So being stupefied, he handed her his company credit card. He sighed after the lady handed it back.

"It went through fine," she said. "I'll give you the keys and it's on the third floor. It's room 201."

***

Oscar entered into his new room and crashed out upon the bed. As to lying there, he wondered on how he was going to find out something big. His eyes were getting sore and blurry, and Oscar sat up to wipe them but they got worse. The journalist strolled along to the bathroom to wash his eyes and face with cold water. Slowly, he returned onto the bed after turning on the ceiling fan. Oscar closed his eyes and thought about calling Lucy, or Amanda; surely, it ought to be Amanda because it was she that got him interested. Yet, Lucy was able to keep his colleagues from telling Stuart about his real lead…

He saw a flock of birds flying directly above his head from the south. He looked around and saw a plume of smoke just two klicks away. He ran as fast as he could knowing that somebody was in harm's way — a low ridge was blocking his view as Oscar overcame it. He looked on and saw an armed-plated vehicle in flames: damn a booby trap. Just near his feet a dead bird fell from the sky…He shot up from his bed that something was in his room. Sun light was coming through the windows and Oscar was the only person in the suite. It became evident that birds were tweeting as he slept. Brooks looked outside and saw some old people sunbathing near a large swimming pool. The guest wanted to explore the place but felt sticky and smelly. He went into the bathroom to freshen up, and put on a clean set of clothes: shirt; shorts and sandals. Before going on his wonder, he thought it'd best to arrange a meeting at the embassy, and headed to the reception area.

***

A girl with a Brummie accent asked, "Good morning, how may I help you?"

"Yes, you may. Can you help me on finding the telephone number for the British Embassy here in Athens?"

"No problem, sir," she said and started typing some details into her computer. After writing onto a notepad, the receptionist gave it to him.

He thanked her and pulled out his mobile phone to make that call. Brooks heard the phone ringing and then it stopped. There was an automated message that advised that he was in a queue so had to wait. Being very patient, Oscar only heard electronica music, and wondered if anybody was going to answer him.

"What kind of service is this?" he asked himself as it seemed that nobody was going to answer his call. Brooks ended his enquiry and returned to the receptionist.

"Hello, sir and how may I help you now?"

"May I have a telephone number for the British consulate, please?"

"Certainly," she said and did the same thing again before handing him that number.

Once more, he thanked her and started to dial. The phone was ringing momentarily before it was answered.

"The British Consulate. How may I help you?"

"Yes, you can," Oscar said, "I want to be routed to the embassy."

"Certainly, just—"

"Before you do anything," Oscar interrupted, "I think you ought to know that the contact number to the embassy is undermanaged. I had been waiting for over half an hour without any joy whatsoever."

"The embassy can get busy during this time of day. I would recommend calling in the evening," the official said.

"That's not good enough. I don't suppose you know that I'm a news correspondent for a newspaper which is very popular for its readers. Are you really informing me that the Foreign Office is actually undermanaged?"

"Just one moment please."

Oscar heard the same electronica music since calling the embassy directly. Nevertheless, the music stopped within five minutes

"This is the Consul-General, Richard Overton. How may I help you?"

"I'm Oscar Brooks, London Eagle. It's very straight forward. I want to book an appointment with the Ambassador."

"Do you now? And what's it about?"

"Clive Roberts, your former Ambassador. We're covering a story about him being a schizophrenic. That's basically it."

"I'm sorry but I just don't understand what that has to do with running this embassy. I'm afraid I cannot be of any help. I heard that you were trying to contact the Ambassador directly without much success. If I heard correctly, you were threatening to expose us as being undermanaged, isn't it?"

"I was concerned that people couldn't get though. However, I think such a report will not be in anyone's interest."

"I agree. Now good—"

Oscar recalled what Amanda had asked him to do. "*Defeat the dark world*, isn't it?"

"...What did you say?"

"You know what I've said: Defeat the dark world," he repeated.

"Look here, young man, do you have any idea who you're fooling around with?"

Oscar responded, "Sure I do. I just want to clear the air for once about Clive's mystery."

"So you want to see the Ambassador, right?"

"Will you set it up?"

"I don't think that it will be a problem. Your name is Oscar Brooks?" He said once he confirmed it, "Let's book you tomorrow's appointment at the embassy. It'll be at two o'clock, and he'll help you on your enquiries. Good day and thank you for showing a genuine interest in our affairs."

Oscar shook his head. *Was it that easy to see the big cheese?* he thought as he paced around the foyer. It was just blatant; the term was sagacious amongst Foreign Office officials. Oscar looked at his watch and it read half-past eight in the morning. Something triggered him about the resort; people do love to sun bathe early! He headed towards the receptionist again.

"I'm sorry but what do you recommend to pass the time here?" Oscar asked.

"Are you looking forward to tonight's bingo?"

"Yes," he lied, "so what do you suggest now?"

"We have a coach leaving this morning to visit the old ruins. If you wish to stay put, there's the pool."

"Thank you very much, when does it leave?"

"Eleven this morning and don't be late," she replied.

Oscar thanked her and decided to take a walk about the resort. It was a very large building and the swimming pool area was now completely jam-packed — it became clear to Oscar that the sun-bathers got their early to claim those beds. Oscar could hear somebody shouting near the pool and he got nearer to the commotion.

"Look here sonny, I went to fetch a banana for breakfast and you took my seat."

"It was vacant," the teenager replied to the older man.

A pool attendant got between them and promised the teenager that he would look for a spare one, and the dispute was diffused. Oscar decided to retired back to his suite to consider on tomorrow. As he was walking, he gathered that he was the odd one out: a lone holidaymaker, but nobody seemed to care about his plight.

***

He was ten minutes early when arriving at the embassy. There were security guards patrolling around as one approached him.

"State your business, sir?"

"My name is Oscar Brooks and I'm here to see the Ambassador," he informed.

"Right you are, he's expecting you. I'll take you there right now."

Oscar felt a cool breeze after being led inside. He noticed the checked marble polished floor, and high columns of pillars supporting the balcony above. Brooks was walking along a red strip of carpet which took him up a flight of stairs onto that floor. The man knocked on the door before asking Oscar to step inside. The room was large and there were many books shelved. At a corner, a thin man was observing him and moved towards him with an acute smile.

"So you must be Oscar Brooks, isn't it?"

"Yes, I'm just here to understand a bit more about Clive Roberts."

He laughed. "I don't think that we've been formally introduced. My name is Robert Hensworth. I'm the British Ambassador in Greece."

"You know who I am, right?"

"Of course I do." Robert added, "You work for the London Eagle and you think that I have all the answers why Clive Roberts went mad."

"It's what my sources are saying," Oscar insisted.

"Then I'm afraid to disappoint you that I worked under him. He was my mentor before he handed in his notice."

"So why did he leave?"

"Because he felt that our interests in Greece will be best managed in Britain."

"What's that?"

"You know full well what that entails, he was writing a book." He paused a moment before he said, "In fact, he was writing his accounts in this very room."

"So you know what he was writing about?"

"He wouldn't tell me," Robert remarked.

"Why?"

"All because he didn't believe that I was 100% supportive of his work."

"Can you explain what you're talking about?" Oscar asked.

"He truly felt that Britain was being sold down the river."

"So he was writing a book about diplomacy in Greece, isn't it?"

Robert nodded. "That's exactly the point but may I ask why you have so much interest for this embassy?"

"That's because I want to *defeat the dark world*," he replied.

The man simpered. "Just what the hell are you talking about?"

"We are looking to expose that dark world," Oscar said. "Your hands are dirty."

"I've no idea why Richard wanted me to see you. So you think that I'm a traitor to our country? We aren't at war with Greece."

Oscar couldn't make any sense on what Amanda wanted to retrieve in Athens. However, he was beaten badly just for contacting her. "As you were saying earlier, Clive thought that Britain was being sold down the river, right?"

Richard frowned. "He was a mad man, you know. I mean he did kill his ghost-writer for selling him down the river, right?"

"I don't want to be rude but I just cannot leave here without any substantial information."

"You must be a little odd. I could call security to get you removed."

"I could expose this embassy that you'd a lunatic running this office; a dangerous official that worked to entrust the Greeks and fellow Britons."

"That doesn't change anything." Robert reacted. He took out a book from a shelf and quickly flipped though. "You haven't a clue why I wanted to meet you here, don't you?"

"I'm here to *defeat the dark world*."

"You aren't making any sense. Just who the hell do you think I am? His psychic?"

Oscar felt troubled. "Why are you making this hard for yourself? I just want answers."

"I don't have any to give if it isn't about this embassy being understaffed," he said. "I'm afraid your time is spent. Please will you leave now?"

He was just about to make his way out before Robert stopped him. "I have been cleaning out my office of his trash." He laughed loudly. "Perhaps, my caretaker may have the answers that you seek!"

It was better than nothing as he left the library. Oscar went to the bottom of the stairs in search of his caretaker. He approached a butler and asked, "May I find the caretaker?"

The butler was alarmed by his response. "You want to see our handyman?"

Oscar nodded. "Yes, Mr. Hensworth feels that he has something of great importance for my news story."

"Fine," he said, "you just wait right here."

"You wish to speak to me, sir?"

Oscar nodded to the caretaker. "Yes, it's about your previous employer, Clive Roberts. He had possessions."

"He did," the man agreed. "Before Clive cleared his office, he left all sorts of stuff behind like parker pens, his diary and a notepad."

"May I have a look at them?"

"You can, sir," he said. "Just follow me into the dining hall. Mind you, Mr Hensworth has those pens now."

The pair walked across the foyer into that room. It only had a long oak furnished table and chairs in the middle. Nothing was laid there and Oscar noticed a speckle of dust when he inspected it with his finger.

"Nobody eats in here these days. Just wait here while I get his former belongings," he said before leaving.

"Here you are sir," the caretaker said after scattering them onto the table. "When you are finished, just inform the butler."

"Do you still want them?"

"Well, I don't want them. I placed them in the storing cupboard where others have left their stuff behind."

Oscar asked, "What other stuff?"

"Things like stereos, walkmans. It's those types of things."

Oscar thanked him and began to look into the diary. It did belong to Clive Roberts and it was over six years old. He didn't find anything of interest; appointment dates with the Foreign Minister, his Consulate appointments and to call his daughter. He checked it again. The book wasn't updated on a daily basis and it was easy enough to browse through it. He noticed Richard Overton's name being placed on the same day with his daughter's; that was the pattern he observed. The other item was the notepad. He turned the page and saw a written passage:

> *Ephesians 6:12 For our struggle is not against flesh and blood, but against the rulers, against the authorities, against the powers of this DARK WORLD and against the spiritual forces of evil in the heavenly realms.*

His stared at two words thinking that he found something big. He flipped the page and he saw further information as if written in one sitting. There was a repeated word: TITAN. *What the hell is this?* he thought. There were names of people attached to the Titan word. Oscar didn't recognise any of them. He took a seat to try to make sense of it all. He turned another page and there was the name Maxwell Spencer having Titan near his name. Oscar could only assume that that person had beaten him badly. He flipped another and saw Richard Overton being titled as a Titan too!

He said aloud, "No wonder he shown interest in the *dark world.*"

He searched every page if Robert Hensworth was enumerated as well. There were many entries but his name wasn't amongst them. *Oh my God*, he thought, *it isn't enough to tell Stuart that I've stumbled on something huge.* Oscar felt something within; a yearning to tear the notepad and smash the room. He seemed indignant that his life was ruined. Yet, the fact remained that Richard Overton's name was written in the notepad; he might have the answers that he was looking for. He held onto it to slip out of the room...

Just as he opened the door, he saw the caretaker waiting outside.

"Did you find what you was looking for?"

Oscar feigned a smile. "No not quite but may you take me to the loo?"

"Certainly, sir."

"No just point me in the right direction."

"Well, it's just past that marble sculpture."

"Thank you, so are you waiting for me?"

"I'm waiting to place them into the storing cupboard."

"I'll leave them with the butler, if that is OK?"

"That's fine with me," said the caretaker and moved on.

When he was out of sight, Oscar made his exit through the front door. On the streets, he walked amongst the vibrant people of Athens. There were cafes, shops and bars on either side. He wanted somewhere quiet to speak to the General-Consul. He saw a sign post that clearly stated museum in English. It also indicated that it was hundred paces ahead. He walked quickly towards it. Just outside, he saw a noisy demonstration with placards and megaphones — the building was closed as people were picketing. He noticed a park sign and headed that way. He changed his mind after a taxi pulled up aside of him. A lady came out and he jumped in.

"I'm lost but can you take me to the Express holiday resort?"

"My English no good, sorry!"

Oscar climbed out of the vehicle. He wandered a little and ended up down a street filled with tourists. On either side, there were postcard stands. Oscar carried on walking until he was at its end. Looking from left-to-right, he still felt he hit the jackpot and aimlessly was going anywhere but back. Oscar clapped in delight when he saw a building situated across the street. It was huge with the sign, CLASSICAL, written above it. There were some banners draped from the high windows too. Oscar crossed the busy road. The Briton felt his luck was changing as to being greeted by a bellboy before entering, and took a seat in the reception area. Oscar could only wish that he could have checked-in at that hotel as it looked grand in many ways: Everybody was in formal uniform; his entrance was well received and it was very cool. Another bellboy smiled at him as he took out his phone to make his call.

"May I speak to Richard Overton? We have spoken yesterday about something affecting the Foreign Office."

"May I take your name?"

"Oscar Brooks."

"This is Richard Overton. What do you want now?"

"I want to talk to you in person."

"We can talk on the phone, it's not a problem."

"We could indeed," Oscar anticipated, "since we're talking about your involvement in Titan. I mean to defeat the dark world."

"What do you think you know about that?"

"So you're willing to talk about that over the phone?" Oscar said amused.

"OK. You may see me in person. Let's say in the next couple of days at my Consulate. It's not in Athens."

"So where is it then?"

"It's on the island of Crete. It's the only Consulate here, and be there four-sharpish."

Oscar heard him hanging up. He now considered if there was anything solid to confirm to Stuart. After all, the notepad was written by Clive Roberts and he did seem to imply that his own colleagues were ancient gods! He moved to the receptionist and asked her to order a taxi to his holiday resort. After that, he reclaimed his seat again to make another call.

"Amanda, hiya, it's me Oscar."

"Oh my God! So you've found something?"

"Yes. Like you said, *come here and the evidence will present itself*."

"Are you pulling my leg?"

"No, I got a list of names of people involved in the Titans. What is it?"

"Let me be frank. You have information that they will kill you for. Am I the only person that you have spoken to?"

"I've spoken to a person with that Titan title—"

"Oscar! You're in grave danger. That's why my father was framed for threatening to reveal those bastards. I remember him telling me that he wanted to expose those that consider themselves gods!"

Oscar looked around and everybody was minding their own business. He got up to wait outside. "You said that I was in grave danger, didn't you?"

"Yes you are. You need to keep that list safe. Get back to London now!"

"I still got four days left out here. Besides, I'm seeing one of the Titans shortly."

"You mustn't see him. He will kill you!"

Oscar laughed. "He's a Consul here in Crete. You aren't telling me that by walking into his building, I won't walk out alive?"

"Just be careful. Where are you staying?"

"At a holiday resort: Express," he replied. "Why? Do you want to see me in person?"

"No! At least you are in a public building but just keep yourself safe."

CHAPTER 8

THERE WASN'T A bellboy welcoming Oscar into his residence. There weren't any reps asking if he was lost in a holiday resort. Furthermore, he didn't have to book a family suite. The day he woke up, it was fairly peaceful and quiet. He took on his reminiscence when he looked below from his balcony, at the resort in Athens, to hear a commotion at six in the morning over a sun lounger! He laughed slightly as it was just too wonderful that the only sound being heard were the birds and insects outside; their fine morning greetings made him wanting to remain in bed for evermore. It felt like heaven; his body had surrendered to not start his day. Oscar also felt spoilt when to think of Capt. Blackwater would have kicked and screamed at him to get out of his recumbent state; he only smiled.

He woke up again and could still hear the greetings outside. *I'm supposed to meet Richard Overton!* He thought and rose from his slumber to stare into a mirror in front of him. He saw behind him an opened window. Oscar turned around to look outside as something startled him. The journalist smelt a strong aroma and moved towards it. As he peeked, Oscar observed a climbing plant covering his side of the wall. He looked beyond the flowers; a bench was facing him across a narrow lawn. Behind that was a little drop which had another building. The landscape around him was of a green forestry and the skies were clear. *How could I not stay here a little longer?* Oscar thought as he lay back upon his bed. He ran in his mind about Amanda: She was truly a gorgeous woman but with a dilemma. The news reporter stirred again and was suddenly on his feet. So towards a washing basin, Oscar cleaned himself up before putting on some fresh clothes. Afterwards, the guest returned a smile as to walk pass a receptionist before reaching the small car park (hiring a car had great importance since everywhere around him was distant). Driving in the afternoon was strangely pleasant and Oscar pondered upon his appointment to match the hospitality behind him. The narrow road ahead of him was mainly straight and traffic was dead quiet, and the only sound heard was the engine of his small Fiat Punto. The road in front eventually changed as it twisted and turned up a large steep hill. It was certainly a hot day but the breeze hitting the side of his face was a relief. He looked upon his watch and it was now half past three. He still had enough time to reach his destination.

***

The building was now straight in front of him as he thought about meeting him. Oscar hadn't a problem finding a place to park his vehicle in Frangokastello, and wandered onwards. Inside, he told a lady behind a desk who he was and whom he wanted to see.

"He's expecting you, today. Please take a seat while I inform him that you're already here."

Oscar obliged to her offer and waited a while before a man stood right in front of him.

"So you must be Oscar Brooks, isn't it?" Richard said, after being acknowledged, "So you say that you want to see me in person so join me in my office."

Oscar followed him along the ground floor and as he entered, it had many ornaments scattered all over the room. He saw an African wooden statue of a warrior at one corner; many Greek vases of ancient dark warriors wearing helmets and carrying spears. There was also a statue of Cronus holding a sickle, and of Atlas.

"Please," Richard said, "take a seat at my desk."

"Thank you," Oscar replied.

"So what is actually bothering you about Clive Roberts?"

"Well, I was running a story on him after the brutal murders of a couple in Hammersmith."

Richard hummed. "Do go on please."

"As you may already know, Clive stated that he wanted to *defeat the dark world*," Oscar said. "He seeks redemption from his dark past," he conjectured correctly.

"He was a very troubled man. But why do you think that I can help you?"

"I came to ask you about what do you know about Titans. It's alleged that you're one of them so will you confirm that?"

"Titans you say," Richard answered. "All I know about that is that there were ancient Greek gods that were set to go to war against the Olympians. You say that I'm a Titan, right?"

Oscar nodded. "You're not telling me that Clive Roberts was wrong, are you? He was a righteous man who does recognise the errors of his ways. He could've remained as such but decided to turn against that."

Richard only hummed again. "If you think that I can do miracles, I bid you farewell."

"My opinion doesn't matter, Richard Overton, it's yours. You have been listed as a Titan and it's alleged that Clive was framed for those murders. Maybe you should double check your infrastructure. Besides, I wouldn't have been here in the first place."

"You're making a grave and unfounded allegation about this Consulate."

"You mean the Foreign Office."

Richard laughed mildly. "I mean that you're making unfounded allegations against the Foreign Office. Did you know that our office is here to help Britons go about their business peacefully in Greece? Also, we keep the peace by using diplomacy here. Oscar, Clive Roberts was a troubled man about ancient gods."

Oscar felt annoyed. "Mr Overton, do you know that I work for the press? The allegations will be out in the open about your involvement as a Titan."

"So why come here if you know already?"

"Because I'm giving you a chance to clear your name!" Oscar responded.

Richard shook his head. "You're giving me a chance," he said, "to find redemption? You haven't a clue what is really going on here, do you?"

"Come clean. I'm sure our government will find clemency in your confession."

"You don't have a clue in what you could be getting involved in. For all you know, I could be doing espionage on behalf of Her Majesty's government. "

"So Her Majesty's government is framing an innocent person on a double murder?"

"That's just what I'm saying. You haven't a clue that Clive isn't as innocent as he's making out."

Oscar was stupefied by his remark. "So you're confirming that Clive was a Titan?"

Richard giggled. "Yes, he was!"

"May I be frank with you?" Oscar now asked.

"About what?"

"I've been investigating the Titans for quite a while now. Clive turned away from the likes of you because he wanted to—"

"You already said that. I'm afraid that you've wasted you journey and I'll be sincere to say this: You must leave me in peace," Richard said. "Just before you leave, how did you come across such information about Titans?"

"Why do you want me to leave all of a sudden?" Oscar asked. "I've only just got here."

"As you may imagine, I'm a very busy man. So I'll ask you again, how did you come across such information about Titans?"

"A valuable source," Oscar said as he got up.

The pair walked a short distance and they made their farewells. Oscar recollected on what he knew so far: Richard Overton didn't seem to deny his involvement. For him to consider that Clive Roberts used to be them; he had to visit him in prison. He continued walking up to his car with a dreadful thought that Stuart was going to let him go. Turning the ignition, he started driving. It was still a lovely evening — despite Richard not making his full confession! He passed a small village where old people sat outside a café enjoying what remained of the day. Oscar saw a Jaguar moving closely behind him. Of course, it seemed odd to see a British expensive car but thought nothing of it. He continued driving through Frangokastello making the necessary turns to find his way home. He looked again into his rear view mirror and could still see the Jaguar tailing him. Brooks was feeling confident to outmanoeuvre in odd situations; he hit the brakes and turned around to see that car...It stopped behind his. He looked around and saw a dozen people walking nearby. The journalist climbed out of his car to approach the Jaguar.

Knocking on the window, he shouted, "Just who the hell do you think you are?"

He got the attention of the locals but didn't get a response from within. The windows were tinted black as he tried to make out who was in there. He kicked the door and shouted again, "Get the fuck out of that car!"

Still he got no response.

Oscar kicked the door mirror and it hung loose. But still, there wasn't a response. He proceeded to get into his own to drive back home. The road was straight until he got to a section where it would twist and turn, downwards, along the face of a large steep hill. Brooks looked into his rear-view mirror and the Jaguar was gaining on him fast. He didn't think much of it so slowed down but the Jaguar rammed him from the side. He stopped and that car was now in front of his.

"What the fuck is wrong with you people?" Oscar shouted and he shook his fist. "Are you insane?"

The Jaguar was moving in reverse, at full throttle, and Brooks was trying to move his vehicle out of the way. Smash! His head flung back which hit the head support with a tremendous force. He looked ahead and the car was pushing his car backwards. Brooks had to improvise; Oscar turned the steering wheel to give way and now it was behind his; he stepped on his accelerator and, of course, the car moved ahead. One could be thankful on making an escape gap but the

Jaguar was moving a lot faster before it was ramming his car, yet again. Then it proceeded to drive beside his to make another hit. It became clear that Oscar's car was a lot lighter than the Jaguar and if that car succeeded: His would go over the side of the road and roll down the steep hill.

He was still shouting, "What the hell are you fucking doing?"

That car was hitting his, once more, and it was too obvious that Oscar was in peril. He deaccelerated and the Jaguar did the same too. Smash! Already, the Jaguar could anticipate that he might allow his car to change its pathway and the journalist hit the cliff face with that Jaguar in front. The assailant moved forward to hit him again, and Oscar tried once more to make his escape. He looked behind and saw it racing towards his. Brooks hadn't a clue on how he was going to go a lot faster and was cursing his car-peddle. Soon enough, the car was getting closer and was side-by-side. Oscar had already noticed a pattern when it was going to hit his — he allowed it. As the Jaguar was getting into position, Oscar slammed on the brakes hard. Brooks' car skidded before turning his steering wheel to avoid going off the road. He looked directly in front and saw nothing ahead, but the edge of a short guard rail was damaged. He jumped out. The driver felt the sharp pain at the back of his neck and walked on in front. He could hear something burning below and took a step nearer along the road. Oscar lent forward and saw the Jaguar upside-down in flames. The man knew that the driver was trapped but wasn't in any condition to help as the fire from the Jaguar was getting a lot worse. Brooks had to cover his eyes after a blinding light, and its noise was deafening too. He covered his ears but it was still ringing after seeing a plume of black smoke. The Briton decided that he couldn't do anything else there and headed back to his car. Just as he got nearer, Oscar saw fire engulfing his engine.

"Oh what the fuck now?"

Luck as it that a truck was pulling up by that car and the driver pulled out a fire extinguisher. Oscar saw the brave man attacking the fire but it was out of control.

"Oi! You!" Oscar shouted at him.

That man saw him waving to move to his location, and saw that the car was beyond saving. He got into his truck and get closer to Oscar.

"You American?" the Greek asked.

"British. I'm from England," he replied.

"Why is your car—"

There was another explosion and they both stared at it. The Greek turned his attention to another black smoke below before facing Oscar. "What happened?"

Oscar shrugged his shoulders. "I really do not know what is going on. I was just driving home from the British Consulate when I was rammed into. The next thing, that car lost control and went over the edge. Then my car explodes."

"What are you?" asked the Greek.

"I'm a journalist," Oscar responded.

The Greek was baffled by his answers. "Are you wanted by terrorists or gangsters, we have plenty here?"

Oscar shook his head. "No I don't think so!"

"I can take you back to the British Consulate. It's not far from here."

"That won't be necessary. But you can take me home, please?" Oscar asked.

The Greek was shaking his head. "That's out of the question," he said, "I see two cars going up in smoke and there will be the need to inform the local police."

"All the police will do is take me back to the British Consulate," Oscar said carelessly.

"So you're a terrorist, isn't it?"

***

Something seemed to snap above Oscar's head; so he made a quick glance. It went dark so nothing could be seen.

"What the hell," he reacted.

There was light in the room again and he sighed. The *guest* saw that there wasn't a clock hanging anywhere. Nevertheless, he read the time on his watch; the only thing that seemed to move in that room was the second hand. He took the time to ponder that the second hand took 1rpm. So in an hour, the second hand would have done sixty cycles. It was pure boredom of sitting there idly. Besides, he was told that he wouldn't be waiting long — was the advice actually that he wouldn't be waiting longer? He was sitting in that room for over two and a half hours and kept his fortitude in a positive state: He was out of harm's way. When he first entered the room, it smelt of strong coffee but now the scent had faded, or he was used to being in there.

Nothing had changed when he noticed that he had stayed in the same room for over four hours. He started to tap on the table yet he stopped suddenly. He looked at the small cubed shaped room: It seemed to be more of a prison without any cell bars (he could leave the room but an officer standing outside would ask him to return to his seat). The walls were orange with a mirror fitted against one of them. Oscar gave the mirror the finger — *who knows what might be watching behind that*, he thought. The light finally fizzled and Oscar could only see blackness.

"Oi!" he shouted.

A ray of light entered the room as an officer opened the door. He spoke something in Greek and retreated. Oscar was in the dark again.

The officer returned with two of his colleagues — hardly anybody spoke in English. After the light bulb was replaced, he said something foreign to Oscar before leaving him alone. Time prolonged and Oscar was having enough of their *hospitality.* Of course, if he was asked to help the police in their enquiry, surely somebody ought to speak English, isn't it? A man joined him.

"Good evening, my name is Dimitris Katsaros. I'm a Detective from Heraklion. I'm brought here because I'm the only person qualified to conduct this interview in English," he said. "What is your name please?"

"Oscar Brooks."

"You're British, yes?"

"Yeah."

"So please will you explain to me what happened along the Serpentine Road?"

"I was going home from the British Consulate."

Dimitris nodded. "So where are you staying?" he asked.

"Vouvas. A bed and breakfast known as Niriida."

"Ah yes, a splendid choice. So what happened on the Serpentine Road?"

"That Jaguar came out of nowhere and it was trying to force my car off the road."

"Do you know why?"

"I don't know why."

Dimitris shook his head. "We know that you've been vandalising that car, isn't it?"

"Yes, I did," he admitted, "but it was following me before I got into a rage."

"So you provoke the driver to ram into yours?"

"I didn't provoke him to drive dangerously along that road!" Oscar said defiant.

"That's OK. I just write a report that it was a road rage," Dimitri said. He got up from his seat. "You are free to go."

"What! You held me here for over four hours just to say that?" Oscar asked.

"That's right. We checked with the British Consulate if you're a known troublemaker, and your passport checks out fine. It also seems that you don't have a criminal record on the Interpol too. So you're free to go," Dimitris confirmed.

"Just wait a goddamn minute," Oscar said shocked, "so what was that fucking car?"

"Please, don't swear at me as I'm only doing my job as an interpreter," he replied.

"I'm sorry," he said regretfully, "but don't you have any idea about that Jaguar?"

He nodded. "It was reported stolen and that's all that I can tell you."

Oscar sensed something foul was at play but what could he do with the Greek police? "I need transport to get home in Vouvas," he said.

"I get the British Consulate to see you, yes?"

"No thank you. But where can I hire another car?"

CHAPTER 9

OSCAR KNEW IT would take minutes. It was getting late in the evening and the dusk had already past. Crickets could be heard as he anticipated on taking his first step into safe haven. He laid down his rucksack before taking a seat. Somebody recognised him and quickly dashed towards him.

"We've been expecting you!"

Oscar looked at the man in front of him. "Do I know you?"

"Of course not! We've been expecting you since yesterday. She thought that you've already forgotten about Benaki."

"I have no idea what you are talking about."

"OK. If you would remember, we were all going to take a trip into Athens to see the Benaki museum. But you wasn't anywhere—"

"Oh I see," Oscar recounted, "I did say that I wouldn't mind sight-seeing. However, I had a pressing matter with the British Consulate."

"You were away for three days."

"I was in Crete to see an old friend as well," he excused.

"I see," the rep said bemused. "There were two men asking for you while you were gone."

Oscar looked around for the odd couple; it was a family resort and it would have only been obvious to spot them. "Where are they now?" he asked.

"They no say but they plan to come back soon, real soon in fact," he said and left him alone.

Oscar was back at the Express. He slung the rucksack over his shoulder and proceeded to make his way to his suite. Everybody seemed to recognise Oscar; families were staring at him as he plodded along.

A woman whispered to her husband as he passed by, "That's him."

Oscar heard but pretended to be deaf.

Another said, "That's him in the paper."

Still Oscar carried on as normal but it seemed that his *car rage* was national news. As a journalist, he couldn't figure out how on earth they knew that it was him. He changed his course and walked towards the reception.

"So erm, I was wondering if I could read some newspapers during the last three days."

"We don't keep newspapers here. We aren't like a five star hotel."

"So may I ask why people are looking at me?"

"It's nothing. There was an article about a road rage along the Serpentine Road. It's a very dangerous road to have a road rage on, and we heard that you were a victim of it. It's just a rumour that has been spreading across this facility," the receptionist replied.

Oscar smiled and made his way up.

***

The water had changed white at a specific point. Oscar was alarmed by the sound of the violent impact too. A man emerged and the water changed white once more; water ran down his face as his head sprung up. He shook himself from left-to-right and rubbed on his eyes to clear his vision.

"You never said it wasn't deep! Oh my arse!"

"Because you never asked," responded a little boy in the pool trying the tread in the water.

A man above was walking towards them and blew in his whistle. "No bombing is allowed!"

Oscar was grinning and moved away. The water around him was preventing him to move at a quick pace than he wished. He got to the edge of the poolside and pulled himself out. Still moving away, he got towards the counter and rested his elbows on it.

"What can I get you?"

"Ice Vodka, please," Brooks replied.

The man opened the glass door of the fridge behind him, took out a bottle and planted it in front of him. "That's 5 euros please."

"Put it on my tab, Oscar Brooks."

"Certainly."

Oscar took a gulp and sighed too.

"That's him," a lady whispered to her female friend.

Oscar reacted in kind. "Hi," he said and extended his hand.

The woman stared at him in horror; she left with her friend. His idea of trying to be a cool guy blew in his face as some men were laughing at him too. Oscar wasn't in a mood to share in their fun but carried on finishing his drink alone. Soon enough, he submerged into the pool and rested on the side; his arms spread along it and his head tilted back; he closed his eyes — he then considered that Stuart would be pleased on his findings.

A man appeared to hover over him. He had a complete set of short grey hair and was slim. He stood there for a while that Oscar opened his eyes. After all, the man was blocking his sunlight.

"Are you Oscar Brooks?" the man said in his European accent.

Oscar got out of the pool and reached for a towel nearby. "Yeah. What do you want?"

"We came here earlier but you were away."

Oscar smiled. "A member of staff was telling me that."

"Can we speak in a quiet place, alone?"

"What do you have to hide?"

"We came here as fast as we could and you better come with us quietly."

He shook his head.

127

"We know that you're a reporter at the London Eagle. We know that you're investigating the murders of a couple and that you came here to find answers."

"Well, I've found the answers that I'm looking for. Therefore, I'm taking on my relaxation on my last day in sunny Greece."

"We really need to talk!" shouted another man beside him.

Oscar had dried himself before winking at them. "There's a bar over there."

"Your room, Oscar," said the first man.

"So you heard about the *road rage*, isn't it?" he asked agitated.

"Yes and we heard about what you've found in that British Embassy."

Oscar gasped. "So what do you want?"

The first one smiled. "All we want is to see that you'll return safely home to London."

The journalist laughed. "So you're friends with Amanda, isn't it?"

He nodded. "Yes," he continued, "she's a special woman."

Oscar still pointed at the bar near the pool. "I still insist to sit at the table over there. It's nice and quiet — besides, I hardly know you."

The two men looked at each other before they agreed. Oscar bought a snowball before joining the others at a table. "As a reporter, what information do you have?"

"My name is Antonis," he said, "and he's Graham."

"How do you do?" Oscar asked.

"Fine thank you," Antonis acknowledged. "We heard that you had a list of people involved in the Titans project, isn't it?"

Oscar frowned not knowing what he had in his suite. "Who are you and what's the Titans project?"

Antonis with Graham was cautious to look around before he answered. "The Titans project has been going on for quite some time now. It began here in Greece which was funded by Britain during the cold war. If I can be brutally honest, I don't know the full details of the project but it isn't good."

Oscar was perplexed. "So as a reporter, you want our paper to expose the Titans project? Yet you haven't a clue what it is, right?"

Antonis shook his head. "So what has been happening to you while you seek the truth? You were beaten badly in London. You were followed closely by agents too, yes?"

"I was also involved in a deadly car chase in Crete," he added.

"So you understand the significance of that list?"

"I don't understand its significance because I don't know what it's about!" Oscar responded.

"Just listen very carefully," Antonis continued, "you're in grave danger for having a list of people involved in the Titans project. They already framed Clive Roberts and they will kill you to prevent exposure."

Oscar shook his head. "So you expect me to give you that list in exchange for my freedom?"

Antonis nodded a little. "Yes," he said, "we're here to *defeat the dark world* that Clive wanted to reveal."

"So why don't you ask him in person?"

Antonis smiled but shook his head. "You expect me to visit his prison to ask about that list? I believe that's closely monitored."

"All prisons are—"

"By Titans Security," he added.

"This sounds far too strange for my liking. I do believe you that there's a dangerous Titans group but what's their motive?"

"It's also rumoured that the Titans project has a breakthrough to manipulate the human mind by the use of a narcotic substance."

"By a hypnosis technique?" Oscar asked.

"Something like that but far more advanced."

Oscar laughed. "I may sound crazy but why should I believe a single word that you're saying?"

Antonis replied, "All because that list has members that will kill you."

"If I go and fetch your list but see your name on it, do I expect you to pardon me?"

"I want to use that list."

"You aren't hearing me," Oscar added, "what if you're working for Titans?"

"After all the stuff you've been through?"

"Look pal, I hardly know who you are? So let's consider that."

Antonis got upon his feet. "You will hear from me soon," he said and gave him his contact details. "I hope you will call me so that we can put the records straight."

Oscar accepted. "You'll probably hear from me."

"No doubt," Antonis said and they left him in peace.

Who the fuck were they? Oscar thought after leaving the bar. He returned to his suite and dialled upon his mobile.

"Amanda, is that you?"

"Yes, why haven't you returned to London?"

"I'll tomorrow. Do you know anything about two geezers, by the name of Antony and Craig, in Athens?" He asked incorrect.

There wasn't an uttered word from her. "Amanda," Oscar said, "do you hear me? Do you know Antony and Craig?"

"No, I don't know such people in Greece," she finally responded.

"It's just that two people came here, in this holiday resort, for my list. I couldn't give it to them."

"Did they not say who they work for?"

"No."

"...That's strange."

"Amanda, I only told you about the list. Did you tell anybody else?"

Amanda hummed. "Yes, I only told a very close associate; we do want to expose that dark world."

"So what is your understanding about that dark world and of its goals?"

"Not a lot I'm afraid," she conceded, "only that my father was framed."

"Why haven't you visited your father?"

She gasped. "Why? It's being run by Titans Security."

"I ought to take on my investigation at them, shouldn't I?"

"It's air tight. You won't find anything," she answered.

"Could it be that the associate of yours is responsible for those two geezers?"

"I would have been told of it," she now replied. "I'm sure of it."

CHAPTER 10

THE QUARTER MOON was shining that evening. Oscar woke up. He was certain that he could hear something outside. Moving towards the balcony, the journalist looked below. There was nothing; his guard was up after Antonis' visit. *Who exactly were they?* Oscar thought as he turned away to rest upon his bed. The noise; it was coming from outside again. Brooks quietly took another peep outside. The pool was lit dim but he could just make out a figure; it was moving behind the silhouette of the swimming pool wall. The hotel guest heard someone talking to be quiet too. Oscar headed into the bathroom and picked up a bar of soap. Splash! He looked to see who could be hiding and a couple moved out from their position looking straight into his direction. Brooks ducked away in time and laughed to himself.

"Hey up, if you think that was funny get yourself down here now!"

Still laughing to himself, Oscar headed back to bed. He reflected upon when he saw Amanda at the court gallery. Of course, she was crying for her father but did she know the murdered couple? But Oscar closed his eyes and fell asleep.

The Reporter had a nightmare about Afghanistan and woke up again. He lied in his bed thinking about his friend being trapped and burnt alive in his SUV...He could definitely hear something still going on outside; it now seemed strange that the romantic couple would be banging into sun loungers, right? Oscar took a peep over the balcony wall and saw the same couple returning back into the hotel...There were also three men walking onwards to the hotel entrance. He moved away to consider who they were? Oscar imagined that something didn't seem right so couldn't just return to bed — He put on a layer of clothes before leaving the suite. Oscar opened the door a little to see if the corridor was occupied at all, covered his eyes to adjust to the landing lights and headed to the stair case exit nearby. As to look down, he heard somebody coming up. The reporter retreated back onto the corridor and wondered if he should make a run to the next stair case. *No time,* he thought since he could only hear one set of feet going up — the other two might be going up the other stairs. Oscar conceded to return to his suite, locked the door and headed towards the balcony again. He looked down and the swimming pool was directly below him — he wouldn't dive as it was the shallow end. Brooks had to climb up onto the balcony above him. Like a cat burglar, he made haste. Oscar waited to hear of any activity coming from his room, his door forced-opened.

"Where the hell is he?" A man said in perfect English.

"I'm sure that he was staying in this room," a second voice said.

"Perhaps he has gone for a night stroll or something daft," said the first.

"We came for that list, so where is it and what will it look like?" the second voice said.

"We'll need to find him first."

Silence followed and Oscar knew once more that he was in danger yet again. He looked through the balcony door and saw a couple sleeping. Brooks looked below and placed a leg over the wall. With both legs over the side, he lowered himself with his arms until his feet touched the top of his own wall. Oscar started a swinging motion to land upon his balcony and looked into his room. The bedside lamp was on and he could see that the door had given in. Oscar proceeded to take his rucksack from under his bed which contained his notepad, wallet and phone. He heard somebody outside and crept towards the balcony...

"There he is! I can see something moving up there!"

Brooks was trying to BE careful but what made him think he was in his room? He hadn't the time to second guess and ran though the suite door towards a stair case. He looked down and heard quick footsteps. Oscar went onto the next floor up. Looking for an obvious escape, he dashed towards an elevator. He called for it and waited, and heard a door from a distance opening—

"That fucker must be on this floor!"

Soon enough, the elevator door opened and Oscar was relieved to step in, but somebody wasn't expecting him. Making a quick assessment on his predicament; he made a chopping-blow on his windpipe. The man was gasping for air and dropped his gun in the process. Brooks pulled him out of the lift and picked up his gun. He pressed to go for the ground floor. Waiting patiently, the doors swung apart and he flitted along the corridor. The intruders weren't visible yet and he saw a woman behind the reception desk. Brooks placed the gun into his rucksack and carried on to leave.

"How are you?"

"Did you not see three men walking pass here?"

"Yes, one of them has a room here, why?"

"Oh its nothing," he said and made his way out of the hotel.

As Oscar left, he heard somebody behind him. Hurriedly, hid behind the bar-stand near the pool, and retrieved his gun and pointed it into the direction of the main entrance. One of the men sped out and was looking into every direction but his. Oscar was now looking along the sight of his gun to aim at him. A second man came out to meet him.

"She said the Brit just took a walk outside," the first one said.

"What a damn nuisance. We could've easily taken him out."

"Where is Alan?" The first asked.

"I thought he was with you?"

Both returned into the hotel.

Oscar looked around to think of where to go next. *Anywhere but here,* he thought and ran out of the complex. As he passed the main gates, Brooks heard some drum noises ahead of him, it was faint and it changed it tempo randomly. He turned around if those men were gaining on him...Oscar ran towards the music in the darkness. Brooks anticipated that the road was a long straight one into Athens. He could see dots of light scattered ahead: Mainly red, white and green. Also, the journalist saw many rectangular-shaped constructions.

The noise was getting louder and louder still but it wasn't coming from there. A car was stationary along the road behind a low wall. A door opened and a young man was speaking not in English. Oscar shrugged his shoulders and kept on running down the road. After a while, he was certain of hearing something behind him; the reporter got off the road and hid behind a shrubbery. Oscar heard the engine running and the loose tarmac being disturbed...He moved onwards.

***

Oscar was the only person carrying a rucksack as he got under the street lights. There were people taking seats along the pavements; drinking and chatting away, others were being congenial too. It was obvious he was on one of the main streets where people were being merry, so could blend with the crowd. Brooks did feel safe but how safe was he really? Somebody was behind him and grabbed him by his shoulder.

"So where do you think you're going?"

Oscar wanted to lurch at him; turned to deliver a punch..."It's you!"

"And it's you!" an old school friend responded. "So what are you doing here?"

"I don't have time," he said and walked away until he saw a dark alley so slipped onto it. Oscar stayed put and considered the odds that those attackers would find him now. He also heard a siren screaming loud then faded. Anyhow, he saw a balcony above a shop and climbed onto the top of a lorry to gain access onto it. Feeling very safe, he lay on the floor and treated his rucksack as a pillow. He felt certain to make a call too.

"Amanda, you were fucking right! I'm shit deep in trouble now."

Amanda was stirring from her sleep. "Is that you Oscar?"

"Of course it's me! I just made the luckiest escape from three gunmen. Gunmen are after me!"

"But you're safe in the—"

"They were paying me a visit," Oscar interrupted. "They were after the list and they wanted me!"

"Oscar, how did they found you?"

"How the hell should I know? Somebody is talking to them. I just know it."

Amanda reacted, "Perhaps they've a much bigger presence than we'd expected."

"I shouldn't have seen Richard Overton. I could've avoided this mess!"

"Calm down," Amanda reassured, "we'll pull through this but you just have to be a lot more careful."

CHAPTER 11

OSCAR HEARD SOMETHING; it was an angel and it shone white. He couldn't understand a word from the heavenly figure and shouted, "Speak clearly for I don't understand what you're asking from me?"

It spoke again but still Oscar was apprehensive. "Please messenger, speak clearly!" The Angel tried thrice but Oscar got jabbed from behind. He turned around but now somebody was hitting him elsewhere...In all awareness, somebody was shouting at Oscar in Greek. He stirred just before he got kicked too. His eyes wide opened, he realised that he had been taking refuge from the gunmen. He was getting kicked a lot harder and was delineated to leave.

"I'm sorry," Oscar said, apologetic too. "My Greek isn't so good."

"My English is good," the man said, "and what do you think that you are doing here?"

"I was—"

He was kicked yet again and Oscar rose to his feet. It was a strange match that the owner was a lot shorter yet feisty. The contrite guest saw the owner returned inside. Since it was during the early hours of the day, Oscar had a chance to look around, and the immediate area was spacious. The entire building was once painted in sky blue but patches were showing its age. Beyond, the ground was newly tiled. It also had Sago palms that were planted in large pots around the vicinity, which Oscar could smell. As he took deep breaths, a police officer was observing him below; Brooks waved at him. "Good morning, it's a wonderful morning, isn't it?"

The officer didn't respond but kept on walking onto the main street.

"Thank fuck for that," he muttered to himself.

Still on the balcony, he saw that the lorry — that he used to climb — wasn't there. The owner re-emerged with a broom.

"My English is very good. Just who-the-hell are you to steal from me?"

"I'm not stealing anything," Oscar responded.

"So what are you doing with that rucksack?"

"It's my clothes. I was just drunk," he excused.

"If you…"

He tossed his rucksack over the side before jumping over onto the street below.

Oscar was still shouted at as he proceeded to move away. "You English have no right to steal where you please!"

There were several people staring at him, and one of them approached.

"Did you steal his meat?"

Oscar quickly opened his rucksack. "Look! No meat!" He closed it promptly as well.

The man who had already glanced into his rucksack was satisfied. "I'm sorry but what were you doing up there?"

"I was sleeping. I got drunk last night and I slept there," Oscar excused.

It was going to be a very hot and shiny day. The streets were busy with a lot of activities: There were market stalls for vegetables, fruits and meat. Oscar could smell sausages roasting and he ordered a hot dog. Whilst eating, he recollected the danger again: The gunmen had planned his execution. Anyhow, Oscar was sanguine that it was safe to return in broad day light.

***

"Good morning, sir."

Oscar recognised the receptionist smiling. "Good morning."

"How has your stay been so far?"

"Fine, I will come back here with my friends from London," he praised.

"That's marvellous," she said still grinning. "There were numerous people asking for you. Even my supervisor wants to have a chat with you."

"I'm checking out. I do have a plane to catch. Surely it isn't anything important, is it?"

"It has to do with your door being breached — one of the holidaymakers reported it to us."

"I panicked last night. When I saw the door damaged, I just went into the night. I'm fine now."

"There was also an incident that occurred on the fourth floor. A man was found lying there with breathing difficulties. He has been attacked and is taken to hospital."

Oscar feigned to be surprised. "Oh that is terrible," he said. "Does anybody know who could've done such a thing?"

"Nobody actually knows yet," she responded.

"Did you not notice anything strange last night?"

The receptionist was confused by his question. "There was a man lying half-dead along the corridor," she now responded.

"I meant anything else?"

"Your door being compromised," she answered.

"I really mean something other than those?"

"...No."

"Nothing?" Oscar asked again.

"Nothing," she reaffirmed.

"Mr Brooks?"

Oscar turned around and saw a woman in a black dress standing a short distance away. "Yes," he replied, "I'm Oscar."

"Can we talk a bit about what happened last night?"

"Well, somebody was trying to burgle me," Oscar replied.

"Was anything taken?"

"Not as far as I can tell," he added. "I think they were after money."

"I'm sorry to hear that but I only hope that we can offer you another suite."

"It's ok," Oscar continued, "I'll be checking out now. Please can you order me a taxi, anyway?"

***

Oscar walked down the steps of the Express entrance. It had a gravelled drive with a huge round fountain planted in the middle of it; at its centre stood a large marble statue of a man wearing a laurel wreath. At the other side of it, he saw two men observing him. Oscar smiled and calmly walked towards his taxi. It sped off! He looked at it going around that fountain before making its exit. The two men smiled back and one of them had already pulled out his gun. *In broad day light,* Oscar thought and ran towards the fountain for cover. He heard something whizzed past him and saw it chipped the hotel wall. Brooks dug into his rucksack to find his gun then he aimed down the sight. Holidaymakers nearby were screaming when they realised that a battle was set into motion. Oscar signalled a warning shot but they fired at his position.

"You're a fool coming here to Greece," one of them said. "You've seen first-hand that people will die for that list."

"What do you want with it?" Oscar asked aloud.

"You're putting many years of hard work to go into smoke. You mustn't—"

"You got balls to blaze guns here!" Oscar remarked before he shot back.

Brooks sensed that they were closing in on either sides of the fountain. He popped on his left before dashing across in that direction. He then fired behind at one of the gunmen who took cover at circular stone structure. Oscar was to make his escape.

***

He ran at a steady pace for over thirty minutes, and at times, looked over his shoulder. All that mattered was to be scarce. Brooks stopped and felt his back drenched of sweat. The reporter saw a bench positioned below a shop window and took rest. He laughed a little that he was in one piece. Oscar hadn't heard his heart beating hard for quite some time, and had trembled when coming to terms of being outgunned. Yet, his escape would be memorable. Looking around, Brooks saw a lot of racks filled with postcards of ancient ruins. A shopkeeper took a seat beside him.

"Are you fine?"

He nodded. "I'm just out of breath. I've been running for almost half an hour," he replied.

"Are you from England?" she asked.

"Yes."

"On holiday?"

"Sort of," he answered, "I'm doing journalism."

"On your own?"

He nodded again.

The shop-owner looked perplexed but smiled. "Rest here and let me fetch you a glass of water?"

He ingratiated her and leaned back. There were a lot of tourists roaming the streets and all Oscar could think about was his narrow escape. The woman eventually returned with his glass of water.

"May I ask you for another favour?"

"What of it?" she pressed him.

"May you order me a taxi?"

"Where will you be going?"

"To the Airport," he responded.

She looked at him from head-to-toe. "Are you bailing out of a hostel?" she seemed to joke.

Oscar could only nod. "Something like that."

Once more, she entered into her shop.

Oscar saw his taxi and thanked the woman for her generosity. The woman was weary that she scurried inside. Regardless, he ventured onwards to his vehicle and on his approach; two vans were hurdling towards him and stopped short. Before he could react, five men cladded in black in combat-wear jumped out shouting. The only thing Oscar could do was to be remained still. They continued to speak in Greek and Oscar figured that he ought to raise his hands. One of them kicked him from behind which brought him down to his knees. He was suddenly lying on the floor, face down too.

***

Oscar sat in a room shackled to the table. Yet again, he would be part of a police enquiry. A clock was on the wall in front of him showing the time 10.30am. It was obvious that he couldn't leave on his will and wondered how long one had to wait for somebody to speak in English. Just like his similar visit, there wasn't much to admire yet he found the floor tiles had a check-square pattern in white-and-grey. Also, a smaller square was added thorough out. *Why should I care?* he thought, *for I could be charged for my troubles.* Oscar only sat in the room for five minutes that the door opened. In came a large fat plain-clothed officer holding a disposable plastic cup of coffee. He sat across him, smiled and took a sip...He was abhorred to the taste that he left the room in an instance.

On his return, he had a wider grin. After he reclaimed his seat, he drank into his mug of coffee. Looking pleased with himself, he put on the tape recorder.

"My name's Detective Vasilis Panagnakos. So you must be Oscar Brooks, yes?"

"Yes."

"So can you tell me what just happened at the Express holiday resort?"

"I was running for my life," he responded.

"From what?"

Oscar answered, "I haven't a clue. I've only came to Greece to do a news story on Clive Roberts."

"And who is that?" Vasilis asked.

"He's a Briton who committed a double murder. He used to be the British Ambassador here, too."

"So what has that got to do with you concealing a dangerous weapon and running from a crime scene?"

"I was running for my life!"

"If you were running scared so from whom?"

"I was attacked last night."

Vasilis nodded. "Yes. But I'll ask you this, why would anybody want to attack you in a holiday resort?"

"Look I heard noises last night near the swimming pool. I had the balcony door opened because it was just damn too hot last night."

"We can pretend that you're not involved in the drugs ring, isn't it?" Vasilis asked.

Oscar couldn't compute. "Are you saying that I was being chased by gangsters?"

"Yes," he said smiling. "There was a man with a damaged windpipe in the hospital that we recognised: A British ex-patriot. He was an enforcer for a crime family in Athens. As such, he was very interested to pay you a visit, eh?"

Oscar still couldn't compute with his revelation. "Are you saying that I just got myself involved with a drug lord?"

"The thing is, my friend, you were being chased by the same gang along the Serpentine Road in Crete, wasn't it?"

"I was following up on a lead to cover my news story," Oscar said.

"Two people left dead and you're alive. Did you attack the man on the fourth floor?"

My DNA! Oscar thought. "Look, he had a gun and it was only in the line of self-defence," Oscar confessed.

"Are you an enforcer? I mean you seem to know where to hit him."

"I used to be a soldier in the British army," Oscar answered.

"So you're a hired gun?"

"I'm a journalist."

"Tell me about Clive Roberts?"

"I've just told you!"

"No you haven't told me why you're actually interested in the murderer."

"He claims that he's innocent. My job was to come to Greece to talk to his former colleagues about him."

"So you did find that he was mixed-up with some dodgy characters, yes?"

"No. I've found that he was losing his mind about the difference between good and evil," he excused.

"You could be charged for the double murders: The Serpentine and at the Express. Do you understand that?"

Oscar hummed. "I hadn't any intention to kill anybody."

"So prove to me why those murdered had to die?"

"I'm not going to say another word," Oscar said.

"So you want a lawyer?"

"I'm not going to be treated like a thug."

"I'll advise the British Consulate on your inappropriate actions over the last 24 hours. As you know, legal expenses are very costly – even for a journalist."

"I don't have the answers that you think I have!" Oscar shouted. "I came here to make an exclusive story on Clive Roberts. Maybe, just maybe, he got mixed-up with the wrong crowd and—"

"So you know who is trying to kill you?"

"I only went to two significant places: The Embassy and the Consulate."

"So if I join the dotted lines, am I to believe that the British government is funding our drug-lords in Greece?"

"Believe what you will! But I have nothing to do with getting involved with drug-lords. Haven't you checked my holiday suite?"

"We're checking it now, sir," he replied. "You can make it easy for all of us if you confess that you're involved in the drugs feud," Vasilis said.

"You mean you want to make it hard for yourself when you find the truth: I'm not involved in narcotics!" Oscar stated.

"I'll ask you again," Vasilis went on, "you're involved in the drugs feud here in Athens; we'd already fifty-six confirmed murders this year. They're all related to drugs and their deaths are terrible; their heads exploded." He paused to stare into Oscar's eyes. "Yes," he continued, "it was the use of bullets that are only found on the black market. Also, it's unlawful since it's breaking the Geneva Convention."

"I have no idea—"

Vasilis slammed on the desk. "That weapon in your rucksack was loaded with exploding bullets! You knew that didn't you?"

"I have no—"

"Tell the fucking truth! You came here not to carry out an investigation but to buy illegal goods."

"I didn't buy that gun as it belonged to that dead man."

"Oh we'll see," Vasilis said. "Why on earth are you making this a lot difficult on yourself? You said that you were a soldier, yes?"

Oscar wouldn't answer him.

"You'll be sent to our Greek prisons for a very long time. Since you cannot speak a word of our language, you better keep one-eye opened when you go to sleep."

"Just who do you think you're?"

"I'm the man that is going to prosecute you in the Greek courts."

"Oh really," Oscar said amused.

"Oh yes, I'll be paying you a yearly visit to see how you're coping with the Greek criminals; and some of them are down-right monsters. You better learn Greek before they treat you like a stack of shit. Just make it easy for yourself and confess to your crimes. I'll recommend a prison with lighter security, OK?"

"No need," Oscar said, "I'll be walking out of here real soon."

CHAPTER 12

OSCAR WAS READING the time on his watch: 9.13pm. He had already missed his flight home and checked the contents of his returned rucksack. Of course, the only thing missing was the gun.

"Oscar Brooks, I don't know who you think you're attracting our drug lords," Vasilis said. "If I'm right, you're very lucky that those gangsters off-loaded your shit. In any case, you should leave Greece for good."

He reacted, "Thank you for your advice."

"I've never heard of a visitor gaining so much heat before. Yes, you're the first."

The forensic team found that there were two types of DNA on the gun: his and the man killed.

Of course, the police couldn't find any narcotics at his suite. They decided not to charge him for murder; holding a concealed weapon and for discharging the gun — Oscar wasn't the man they wanted on drug violations. Walking along the street aimlessly, he signalled a taxi.

"To the airport please."

"No problem."

***

Oscar was able to book a flight back to Britain that evening. The flight itself wasn't eventful and was looking at his new found list over and over again.

"What are the Titans," he whispered to himself.

"They were Greek gods that declared war on Zeus and his Olympians gods."

Oscar turned to his right, in his seat, at the gentleman beside him. "Of course," he said, "I was just thinking out loud."

"It's not a problem," the man said, "It beats humming to myself before arriving at Heathrow."

Oscar nodded.

"So," the man said, "you went to Greece on business?"

"I was there to do some journalism."

"So you heard about the shoot-out at the holiday resort? A man got killed."

"I heard about that," Oscar answered.

"Nowhere is safe in Athens these days due to the drugs feud. Anybody can be picked off."

"True."

"So what news were you covering?"

"The British embassy, just how it's under-staffed," he hoodwinked.

"Really?"

Oscar nodded. "Really."

"So where do you work?"

"The London Eagle...At the moment."

"So I should be able to read your report?"

Oscar nodded again.

"It's nice meeting you anyway."

The man placed on his sleep mask and tilted his head back. Oscar was still awake recollecting his visit; the incidents on the Serpentine Road and at the Express that Richard wanted him dead. Oscar was ambitious to run it all for the front cover story.

***

Coming out of Heathrow Airport, he looked around; nobody was following him. Oscar found a payphone and approached it. Before he slipped in a coin, he remembered his mobile in his pocket.

"It's me Oscar, I'm back in London."

"You are here? Great!" Amanda said, "We better meet up pretty sharpish. Meet me at the Roxy nightclub."

"Where?" Oscar asked.

"Just jump into a taxi," she said before hanging up.

A taxi rank wasn't far and he got into one of the cabs.

"Roxy Nightclub, please."

The cab driver turned around amused. "You wanna get pissed tonight?"

"I'm meeting a friend."

"Cor blimey, must be a great friend of yours. I mean I usually take all of my passengers home. You're the first!"

It was exactly what Detective Vasilis Panagnakos told him. The first to do stuff that nobody else would dream of doing. Oscar only hoped that Amanda could tell him why he was in danger. He knew little about the Titans and was shaking his head in disbelief.

"Had a rough flight?"

Oscar replied, "No not at all."

"You look tried, mate. You should call it a night."

"I'm meeting a special friend that's all."

Cab driver laughed as he looked into his rear view mirror. "Your girlfriend, isn't it? Oh ain't you the saucy devil!"

Oscar grinned. "It's just business," he responded.

The driver winked at him. "You mean one of those escorts?" he asked. "You're still a saucy devil in my books!"

"How far is it?" Oscar asked.

He laughed again. "It's a good blimming fifteen miles away," he said. "This will cost you an arm and a leg!"

"How much do you reckon?"

"It's about 70 quid just to get there. You do have the money?"

Oscar checked his wallet. "Yes I have the money."

The driver smiled. "I should've told ya that when you jumped into my vehicle," he said. "It's just rare, you know."

***

Oscar finally ventured through the front entrance but had irksome that there weren't much security. Also, there was hardly a queue forming outside. It felt peculiar that he wandered out onto the street to read the sign above the door: Roxy Nightclub. *Is this really straight forward?* he doubted in his mind. In any case, Oscar did go in; cautious too. It had double doors and he opened one of them. As he stood inside, he saw the reception with its cloak room to his right and a bouncer guarding another set of doors.

"Six pounds to be admitted," the assistant said to him.

He obliged and paid a further six pounds to store his rucksack.

The bouncer then allowed him access. "I hope you'll have a lovely evening," he proclaimed.

After acknowledging him, he took several steps. What he saw was a cosy small joint. It had the club's name written against a brick wall. At a corner a pianoforte was visible yet nobody was set to play it. There were tables candle-lit and people were amongst themselves enjoying their evening. He could also hear jazz music in the background. It had truly a soothing atmosphere; and for Oscar, nobody would really want to care on what he had been through. *How could I attempt to relax here?* He shook his head that she had underestimated the Titans. Some people had already noticed him standing at the double doors. Of course, he was looking for her but she wasn't anywhere in sight. He went to the bar and it remained odd to him that the club was only ideal for romantic couples.

"What are you having?" the bartender asked.

He doubted the place having his Newcastle Brown but ordered it.

"We don't serve that here," he replied.

"Vodka Ice?"

"Yep!"

"What are you doing?" Amanda asked.

Oscar sipped his drink. "What do you think?"

"We don't have time for you to—"

"Listen here missy," Oscar interjected, "since going to Greece, I got involved in a dangerous car chase, a gunfight and I was arrested twice. So don't you tell me on what I can and cannot do."

"You need to get a grip on yourself," Amanda said. "We need to leave."

"I've just got here," Oscar said. "I haven't had a decent drink for days."

"You do remember the Titans?" she asked.

"It can wait," he said and took a larger gulp.

"Wasn't you followed?" she now asked.

"Not that I can see. They'll know that I'm in London so fuck 'em!"

"What the hell is wrong with you?"

"I just killed a man last night in Greece, and he was a known British ex-patriot to the police. I could've still been in Greece facing a murder charge. But they're more concerned in catching the bigger fish," he said.

"So you're drinking your sorrows?"

"I'd killed a man last night. I left the army because I've killed plenty during my tour in Afghanistan. This isn't the life that I wished to pursue."

Amanda slapped him across his face. "You arrogant bastard!" she said. "I thought you were built for this!"

"Built?" Oscar asked. "I was just following up on a story about your father. I mean what is to stop me doing a report that your father was deranged about his subordinate staff being gods?"

"So you've already forgotten about that list that you're carrying?"

Oscar pretended to fetch something from his rucksack. "You want it?" he asked, giggled a bit as well. "Here have it!"

"What is wrong with you?"

"Let me tell you again. Those fuckers are after my blood!"

"That's why you have to be careful on whom you give the list to," she said.

"Give the list to whom?"

"To an associate of mine; his name is Graham Hopkins."

Oscar was stupefied by her remark. "Was he the fellow that was in Greece?"

"He didn't say that he was actually in Greece. What are you telling me?"

"Two men approached me at the holiday resort: Antony and some other guy. So I do think that *some other guy* is the person that you're speaking about."

She responded, "But Graham was in...I told Graham that you were staying at the resort. And that you had the list....I don't think he's a—"

"You have somebody telling the fuckers on my whereabouts. Oh the bad news is that I'll have people now knowing where I actually live now! So how am I going to have a life of peace and fucking tranquillity?"

Amanda held onto his hand. "You've been brave to pursue the truth; very brave indeed. You just have to remain strong just like my father."

Oscar hummed. "Of course I'm fucking headstrong! But the fact is that I could wake up one morning by a heap of gunmen storming into my apartment — it happened in Greece."

"This isn't Greece," she said.

"What about that night when they took my phone?"

Amanda was still holding his hand. "We'll pull through—"

She felt her lips being pressed by his. She widened her eyes to see his reaction. Oscar's eyes were closed and caressed her cheeks with his hands. He let her go. Amanda stared at him and was preparing an open hand to strike him again. Yet Oscar held her arm.

"Look here missy, I just don't like being taken for a mug."

"How dare you!" she shouted.

"How dare you come here wanting just to take the list from me," Oscar insisted.

"We're a team, aren't we?"

Oscar held her cheeks again and drew her face closer to his. He gave her a deeper kiss and she didn't resist. He started to hold her by the hands and was pressing himself onto hers. Oscar decided to pause a moment.

"You're gorgeous," he said.

"You're a—"

Oscar kissed her again, and wanted to take her away from the nightclub.

"No!" Amanda said. "We still got a lot of work to do."

"OK," he said, "so after we see Graham, we'll be home dry, isn't it?"

"There is something that I should've told you earlier," Amanda said.

"Like what?"

"As you know, my father was trying to expose them. The problem is that we don't have the full details on what it is. One person claims it's about mind-manipulation, and the other may say it's about certain weaponry. But my father knew something."

"So why don't you ask him?"

"Are you forgetting how dangerous it is for anyone to make any revelation? My dad wouldn't tell me because he feared for my safety and others as well."

"So you got me to do your dirty work?" Oscar asked.

"I didn't tell you to meet up with them directly. I mean," she went on, "what got into you?"

"He was trying to make me go around in circles. I just had to see him that he has been foiled."

Amanda shook her head. "Foolish. You knew about my dad and you were a victim of a brutal attack outside your apartment. So you think it was really my fault?"

Oscar smirked. "So you think it's my fault for being a journalist?"

She nodded. "Who else could there be?"

"So where is this Graham fella?"

"I'll see him tomorrow. Just give me the list and I will pass it on to him," she answered.

"Wait just one goddamn minute!" he exclaimed. "You aren't seriously expecting me to just hand over my security blanket?"

"What from the Titans?"

"From anybody!"

"It's a lot more sophisticated than it seems. The list in the right hands will mean that the Titans won't see you as a direct threat."

"And how do you know that?"

"It's my father," she confessed, "he was part of a movement that was totally against the Titans."

Oscar had his arms folded and hummed too. "Out with it girl!"

"My father was part of a small movement known as God's Angels."

Oscar laughed a little. "He could've come up with something a bit more dramatic. What's wrong with calling it Angelic?"

Amanda looked hard at him. "The movement will save your life. Once that list is in their hands, the word will be out that you no longer have it."

Oscar was still smirking a bit. "So you expect this Graham to be immune to being attacked left, right and centre?"

"Well at least you won't need to fear for your life."

"I fear Stuart more." He observed Amanda had been looking hard at him then rolling her eyes in disbelief. Oscar continued as well, "He's my editor at the London Eagle. He'll want to know what has been happening in Greece. I just have to show him the list."

"You're fucking out of your mind."

"It's all good. I show him the list tomorrow and soon enough, I'll hand it over to you."

"I cannot believe that I'm hearing this," she said alarmed. "You called me this evening to say that you'll be taking this up with your editor?"

Oscar nodded. "You've summed it up correctly. But I wanted to see you about the danger that—"

"You've really lost your senses. So you're going to get your editor involved in all of this heat?"

"I've already told you the reason why I went to Greece in the first place; I was to obtain information related to your dad. It turns out that being a journalist has paid off."

Amanda asked, "So who was your source in the embassy?"

"An unlikely candidate," he answered.

"So—"

"As you were saying, I shouldn't get people involved that could get themselves in danger. I shouldn't tell you."

Amanda shook her head. "God's Angels won't be taking this news lightly."

"So what can that group do?" Oscar wondered.

"It was set up by my father and his friends to reveal to the world how corrupt they are."

"It seems that you don't need to be a member of God's Angels to understand that," he said.

"The Titans knew that you're resourceful to our cause. Just hand me the list, Oscar," she pleaded.

"I told you what I was going to do. I'm going to see the big cheese and you'll just have to wait."

"So you're just going to return to that apartment of yours?"

"If I had decent protection, yes I will."

"So where will you be kipping tonight?" she asked.

"Obviously," he sniggered. "It won't be at yours."

Amanda held his hand again. "You just have to trust me that—"

Oscar giggled. "Trust you say? There's a leak in that movement," Oscar said. "Somebody is informing the Titans on where I was—" He stopped short. "But I didn't tell you my room number in the hotel."

Amanda responded, "If you didn't tell me of your room number; the leak came from you."

"I told no one."

"Maybe the bellboy was naughty," she exaggerated.

"So the Titans have a great influence in the hospitality sector too?"

"Not that I'm aware of. Anyway, I told you that you need to be extra careful on how you carry yourself about. Now you'll have to be extra vigilant," she said.

Oscar took another swig of his drink before Amanda got up. "So where you think you're going?"

"Home it seems," she said. "I have no purpose to stay-up with you tonight."

"It comes with the territory on being a journalist," he said. "Come on! Don't you understand?"

"It's your call. Graham isn't going to be happy when I tell him that the list will be handed over to your editor."

"He'll get a copy," Oscar remarked.

"And if he wants the original, you will say nay?" she asked.

"Stuart is a good man, and I work with some magnificent colleagues."

Amanda shook her head once more. "You expect me to believe that? *Your magnificent colleagues* of yours understand the pain it took to get that list, isn't it?"

"Well I did understand your pain so why can't they understand mine?"

"It's because you took me as a fool about *defeating the dark world*. When I rang you, the Titans

174

were assessing you on how much of a threat you are to them."

"All is forgiven, I'll see him tomorrow," Oscar said before finishing his drink. "Any chance," he continued, "that I could kip on your sofa?"

CHAPTER 13

THE TRAFFIC WAS AWFUL that morning; there were loads of road works along the way. Time was money and Oscar imagined that he would be paying time and a half as his fare increased as it stood still.

"We are here," the cab driver said after pulling up. "That will cost you £128.50."

"That's not a problem," he said and paid him handsomely. "Keep the change, sir."

Oscar had his rucksack close and proceeded on inside the Glass House. A security guard approached him.

"May I see your pass, sir?"

He showed him his and ventured into an elevator. Oscar could hear somebody muttering behind him—

"I'm sure it was that person, you know, the one that we're hearing about these days."

Another joined in. "I'm surprised about the whole episode."

The doors swung open and the people behind him left to be on their third floor. One of the ladies had a good look at him and Oscar smiled — she dashed on forward. He was in the lift alone and was waiting for it to take him onto the sixth floor. As the doors opened, he took one step out and everybody recognised him. Regardless, Oscar was a professional like everybody else there and carried on ahead. He was a yard away to knock on the editor's door that it opened.

"Oscar! I'm glad that you can join us! Come in, please," Stuart said with a warm heart.

"Thank you, sir."

Stuart pointed to where he was going to sit — the dreaded sofa — and sat on the other side.

"So what did you find in Greece?"

"I found some of his writings: a diary and a notepad," he answered.

"And you're expecting our chairman just to marvel at his diary and notepad?"

"I do expect to explain them," he answered and placed them on the coffee table.

Stuart examined them quickly and lent back. "What are those?"

"What he wanted to get published."

"I just had a quick look into his diary and it only says something about telephoning Amanda. What its significance?"

"The diary is hardly used by the author but the notepad," he said. Oscar opened it to show him his list of Titans.

Stuart moved forward. "All that I can see are names and the same word next to theirs: Titan."

"That was what I thought," he remarked, "but I carried on thinking on what Sebastian was telling me." He turned a page with the biblical passage about the *dark world*. "You see that?"

Stuart took another look. "Hmm. It's what he wanted to talk about in his trial."

"Exactly, so Clive Roberts was definitely thinking about the dark world after his succession as an Ambassador. We can make a story out of this."

Stuart just stared at him. "It's true that we could run a story that Whitehall employed a mad man but I'm afraid that you won't be running it."

Oscar froze. "I did what you ask me to do. Why are you not allowing me to get this published?"

Stuart sighed. "It's what I've heard what you'd been doing. The rumour is that you were involved in a deadly road rage along a jagged road, isn't it?"

Oscar nodded. "I was following up on an investigation in Crete. Some guy just lunged at me."

"I also heard a report that in the road rage, a person was killed, is that correct?"

Oscar nodded again.

Stuart hummed. "What were you doing in Crete if the man in question was working in Athens?"

"That's simple," he said. "There was a former employee of Clive Roberts that I wanted to see."

Stuart asked, "So what you're telling me is that all of Clive Roberts' former employees are now working in Crete?"

He shook his head.

"Now then," he continued, "I heard an amazing story that you got involved in a gun battle, is that even correct?"

He nodded his head again.

"There is a drug feud going on in Athens and you were having a shoot-out with a local gang, is that right?"

"It was self-defence," Oscar responded.

Stuart's eye brows didn't twitch a bit. His eye wouldn't shy away on Oscar's adventures in Greece. He only bit his lower lip and was still staring at him. Stuart folded his arms and was wearing a dark grey suit and red tie. "It amazes me that you aren't the story than Clive Roberts. Did you know that none of the British papers and the media made you yet? Don't you find that weird?"

"Maybe, because there was a bigger fish to fry, right?"

Stuart shook his head. "You do understand why I cannot have you writing anything further on Clive Roberts?"

Oscar now shook his head. "I don't truly understand, sir," he replied.

"That's because once you start making an exclusive on Clive Roberts, there will be other papers making their own news about your involvement with gangsters, car chases and getting arrested twice!" he shouted.

Oscar nodded.

"If I heard the rumours correctly, the police would've charged you for the murder of a man coming out of an elevator. But since he was a violent and known criminal, you were slap on the wrist!"

"That's true, sir," Oscar responded.

"I cannot have you running the story about Clive Roberts," Stuart said. "But you did good out there."

"So who is going to take the credit for it?"

"Lucy. I want you to put her into speed about Clive Roberts. If it becomes necessary, she will be going to Greece to patch up your story."

Oscar was stunned. "What! Seriously?"

"Seriously, I want you to pass on that diary and notepad to her. Do you get it?"

"So you want me to work with Lucy who'll take all the credit for being a correspondent?"

"Having your name beside her will only spell trouble," Stuart answered. "Our rivals will be stealing our own readers, and I just cannot allow those bastards any satisfaction. Besides, it's purely business."

"Shall I go now?"

"No, not just quite yet," he responded. "Don McQueen will be paying a visit this afternoon. I want you and Lucy to meet him in person."

"Who's—"

"He's the chairman of our paper, London Eagle," Stuart interrupted. "Now meet up with Lucy."

Still people were staring at him as he walked out — people would stop what they were doing and whisper to their fellow colleagues.

***

"Oh my god! It's you!" Lucy said astonished.

Oscar grinned. "Did you miss me?"

She overruled. "What kind of stupid question is that? I mean are the rumours true that you were arrested for carrying and concealing a weapon?"

Oscar sat on her desk and was able to see that everybody was still staring at him. He moved to take a seat beside her to break their line of sight. "Yes, the rumours are very true."

"I think that I should run a story on you," she reacted. Lucy was pointing at her computer screen. "This type of bullshit is just darn dull and boring. Let me run a story on you/"

Oscar laughed. "Only if Stuart will give you the green light," he replied. "Stuart wants you to run the Greece story."

"Really? That one of our journalists—"

"No on Clive Roberts. Stuart wants you to pick up the pieces; I'll be helping you."

Lucy was puzzled by his revelation. "Just wait a minute, he wants me to—"

"I sat on that dreaded sofa. He doesn't want me to run it."

"Oh!" Lucy responded. "Otherwise he would have given you the boot — perhaps you were gaining too much attention from our predators."

"Exactly."

"So what do you have?"

Oscar revealed the diary and the notepad. "It's all in here. It's all of Clive Roberts' visions of the dark world when he was an ambassador. But I think you will need to be careful on how you use the term *dark world*," he said.

183

"Just what are you going on about, the devil?"

Somewhat, Oscar hummed.

"What's going on? Did you find god in Greece?"

"I did study the Bible a bit, and I suppose, I did miraculously come to terms with God," Oscar claimed.

"Amazing," she said. "Did you realise that Clive Roberts was a devout Christian. Didn't he also find god in Greece too?"

"Stop playing with my mind," he objected. "You have a story to run but you just got to be appreciative of the Christian faith, alright?"

"I bear that in mind," Lucy acknowledged.

"Stuart also wants us to meet up with Don McQueen," he added.

***

Don McQueen was smiling to Lucy's presentation. "That's wonderful," he said. He clapped his hands. "I want to see this on the front cover as it will do us some good that London news is what will affect the world. Great work Lucy."

They were all on the sofa in Stuart's office. "That's exactly what I've said to Lucy. She'll be our star reporter when it goes viral."

Don was observing Oscar. "And how does he fit into the equation?"

"He has knowledge on the actual Clive Roberts trial. He had aided Lucy to understand the dark world."

Lucy agreed, "Yes, it's absolutely true since Oscar here is a devout Christian who understands the dangers of the devil."

Don looked bemused. "The devil?"

"Clive Roberts," Stuart added, "was a religious nut that went on a crusade against his ghost-writer and her husband. It seems that he would have harmed his former employees too, if they didn't agree to his way of things."

Don was holding the notepad in hand. "This is great. We can tell the whole wide world that we have evidence on his further demeanour. So when will it be in print?"

"It will be next week Monday. I thought that you better hear it first before we get it published."

Don nodded. "Do it," he said. "I got to get going since I have another pressing appointment."

They all rose from the sofa and said their goodbyes to their big boss.

Stuart was jovial. "I really like what you're doing Lucy. I want that exclusive ready by Saturday, OK?"

"That won't be a problem, sir."

"Here," he said handling her that diary and notepad, "knock 'em dead!"

Both Oscar and Lucy departed from his office.

"He wants to ruin me," he whispered to her.

"I thought you said that he wants to put the lid on the gun battle?"

"It's just the way he addressed you as the *most magnificent employee* — I being the worst."

Heading onwards to the elevator, Oscar recognised somebody.

"It's me Duncan, do you remember me?"

Oscar nodded. "Yes, we spoke about that horrific mugging," he replied.

Duncan muttered, "Is it true that you were involved in a shoot-out?"

Oscar nodded again. "Yes, I was a mistaken identity of being a drug lord."

Duncan held Oscar by his shoulders. "That's just terrible," he said. "If you would like, we can discuss this in the pub."

Oscar smiled before entering the empty lift with Lucy. "Thanks."

"You do know," Lucy said to Oscar in the elevator, "that he's gay."

"I kinda figured that one out," Oscar responded.

"You're a hit with the hunks," she added.

Lucy with Oscar went to her cubicle. She took her usual seat to face her computer but swirled around to front him. "Just what the hell is actually going on here?"

"What do you mean?" Oscar asked.

"So you wanna play dumb with me? So you thought that I've already forgotten about that Bentley; the one that was following us around. As you were saying, *Bentleys are rare and damn expensive*. You were also a hot pursuit in Greece, wasn't it?"

"The cars weren't the same."

"We were followed and it happened to you in Greece. Tell me this..." She now held the notepad and diary in her hand. "What is this really? I've already looked into it and it speaks about the Titans. In case you haven't figured it out, they were ancient gods that were condemned to live in the underworld."

"You know better than I do," Oscar said.

"The underworld means the dark world," she added. She pointed at the list of names. "These names have the Titan title. Did you meet one of them?"

Oscar pointed at one of the names. "I met him, Richard Overton."

"So why does he want to kill you, is it because you threatened to go public that you understood him?"

Oscar nodded.

"Why don't you," she asked, exaggerated, "do an investigation on the Mafiosi? I don't suppose you've heard of them?"

"Of course I heard of them," Oscar responded, irksome too.

"So you think you can just threaten anyone you please because you stand for the good of the people and get away with it?"

"I never thought that I was in trouble. I didn't know exactly who they were," he replied.

Lucy shook her head. "I know you better than you know yourself. You wouldn't have gone to Crete, or

Athens without something digging at you, isn't it? Was it your old friend Sebastian?"

"Sebastian only mentioned about the *dark world*. He didn't know anything about the Titans."

"So he was only representing his client because he had a lot of money, right?" she asked.

Oscar nodded once more.

"And since," Lucy asked, being sarcastic, "Stuart doesn't want us to glamourize your sweet little friend, Sebastian, he doesn't want to be friends with you again, isn't it?"

Oscar agreed.

"So what provoked you to go to Greece, Amanda's mother?"

"I used the term *defeat the dark world* in my report. Of course, I met Clive's daughter who claims that his father was innocent."

She laughed. "So you fell for her looks and believed her, wasn't it?"

"Alright Lucy, she deliberately called me on her tagged phone. By that, those thugs took my phone to see who I made contact with."

Lucy giggled. "So Sebastian is now on their radar," she said. "Have you, by any chance, told him about *defeating the dark world*?"

"I will soon but look here Lucy. It's no good going high and mighty when a lot of stuff has been happening in a short period of time. So why didn't you show your concerns earlier?"

Lucy shook her head again. "If I understood what I know about *defeating the dark world* now, I would have."

"So you do understand why I don't want you to use that term in your report, right?"

Lucy was rolling her eyes at him. "Duh! And you'd found god while you were away in Greece, really?" She kicked him softly on the shin. "Where are you staying since you got back to London?"

"Anywhere that isn't Greek," he replied.

CHAPTER 14

OSCAR SAT CALMLY by the window; it had been a while since meeting-up with Amanda. He loved drinking tea there. It was something that they do during the brewing process; it was majestic according to him. The tea that he made at home, using different brands, wasn't like theirs. Once in a while, he would ask them how they got the perfect refreshment, but they teased him that it was a close-guarded family secret. Being in the café, it served food too, which were usually beans, sausages and chips. Besides his love of the tea, he was congenial to the layout as well. It had been revamped from the days when the chairs were bolted to the floor, and plastic table cloths were used. Nowadays, the chairs were replaced with free standing ones and orange cotton table-cloths. He would dare imagine that it was a splendid tea house — which the establishment wasn't really. He was taking in the view outside and saw his workplace looking grand amongst the landscape.

Along the street, a clothing, bicycle shop and banks were opened in old Georgian buildings. People were shopping too. Taking a sip, he could see her coming with company too. "Who's he," he muttered.

Eventually, Amanda arrived with her friend. "This is Graham," she said after they all sat near the window.

Oscar recognised him. "Are we fine to sit here?" he asked.

"We should be OK," she answered.

"The Titans spell trouble, don't they?" Oscar now asked.

She nodded.

"That's absolutely true," Graham agreed.

"I do remember you in Athens. You wanted to take the list from me?" Oscar asked.

He hummed in thought and nodded. "Amanda told us that you had substantial information to expose the network. I and Antonis knew that you were staying in the Express Holiday Inn. We tried to see you but according to my understanding, you were in Crete, wasn't it?"

"Yeah, I went to see a Titan and now he wants me dead."

"You should consider," Graham continued, "that the list is best placed in the right hands, do you still have it?"

"Yes I still have it and we're going to run a story on the Titans," Oscar confirmed.

Graham smiled and nodded. "How did you convince your paper about the *dark world*?"

"It helps," Oscar added, "if you know the right people in the business."

"That's good. That's very good but not enough to stop the Titans," Graham warned.

"He's right," Amanda said. "The Titans," she continued, "need a push not a wagging finger."

"So how terrible are they?" Oscar asked.

"They're dangerous — if that what you wanted to hear. It strikes me that your paper will like to make allegations on the Titans. They've an auspicious business which has a very close relationship with our British government. So what do you know?"

"We know that they see themselves as the devil," Oscar said.

"What does the list also say?" Graham asked him.

"It says a lot of things," Oscar carried on, "about Richard Overton and the likes. Exposing them should bring down the entire network. The coverage will be in Monday's edition. As a journalist, I've done what is required to get inside the belly of the beast."

"Personally, I don't think that your paper should run with the story. I mean look at you, beaten up in a dark alley; a car chase and gun battle. How can your editor not realise that?" Graham asked.

"My editor only cares about the reputation of London Eagle. This will make the paper the London paper," he responded.

"But danger presents itself in many different ways. I hear you're back in your apartment, is that where you think the list will be safe?"

"I'm not writing the story. We got somebody else to expose that," Oscar answered.

Graham's eyes widen. "Your editor understands?" he wondered. "He understands about the threat the Titans have on this world?"

"Why else will the London Eagle be rolling it on Monday?"

"So why aren't you doing it?" Graham quizzed.

Oscar thought for a moment. "My editor feels that I should only research into the story."

"He feels that you are not up to the task, really?"

"My editor feels that our rival papers will blow it out of proportion. You heard what has happened to me in Greece, right?"

"Who hasn't?"

"If I go public on the Titans then our rivals will go public on me."

"It seems that you've a very understanding employer. So you agree with him?"

Oscar nodded.

Amanda said, "We want that list, Oscar."

He looked at her. "The editor has it," he lied.

"Oscar," she continued, "that list is what we require to bring the fight to them. We need it."

"You'll get your names by Monday," he replied smiling.

Graham with Amanda looked at one another before facing Oscar. Graham shook his head. "So you really think that the list will go live?"

"Of course, *defeat the dark world* do you remember? Everything is now under our control."

"I only hope that you're right, Oscar," Graham said before he got up from his seat.

Amanda held Graham by his arm then both turned to face Oscar. "I sure hope that you know what you're doing."

"So Graham," Oscar started to ask, "are you part of God's Angels?"

"That's true and so is Amanda," he replied.

"I was thinking about that breach in my suite, I don't suppose you know anything about that?"

Graham was abhorred by his question. "What are you implying? That I had something to do with that?"

"It's only a speculation and I'm looking at all avenues," he now replied.

Amanda felt troubled. "So you think that God's Angels has something to do with hiring a group of thugs to take you out? If you want to make ridiculous allegations, then try the same on your editor!"

"That's not fair," Oscar said. "I've kept my stay low-keyed. The only person that I've told was—"

"Me you bastard!" she said. "I told him also."

"And we met at your resort but you thought that I work for the Titans," Graham added.

"So who is Antonis?"

"He's the leader of God's Angels," Amanda responded.

"So why isn't he here?" Oscar asked.

"Ah, Antonis has other matters to attend to," Graham answered.

Oscar drank from his cup before he looked up at him. "More important than the list it seems?"

"Why are you being a tight arse?" Amanda wondered.

"Maybe I'm not getting the groove on becoming part of God's Angels...So what of it?"

"It's a small group that is trying to infiltrate the Titans. What we want is a better society," Amanda replied.

Oscar smirked a little. "But we don't know exactly what the Titans are doing, don't we?"

"My father is in prison for murders that he alone didn't commit. I trust my father and I've learnt that there is something out there trying to manipulate us."

"I do believe you but we haven't a clue what they're manipulating, don't we still?"

"That's why we need to infiltrate the Titans," Graham confirmed whilst he stood.

Amanda seemed to want Graham to say something to him. He was reluctant but he sat down again before he gasped. "Now you listen very carefully. Amanda does care about your safety and the Titans may take advantage that you're vulnerable in your home."

Oscar laughed. "I bought a cricket bat just for the sake of it!"

"That will do no good against a gun. Haven't you forgotten already that dark alley?"

Oscar only nodded. "It's hard to forget that," he replied.

"You should consider this," he placed a little leather case onto the table, "to the letter." He passed it towards Oscar. "In the case is a pistol."

Oscar opened it a little and saw it. He looked up at Graham. "You're expecting a lot of commotion?"

"I expect the worse to happen," Graham responded. "To the letter, use that gun when you sense danger at home. I only carry one around if things get out-of-hand."

"When do you carry one?"

"Just keep the gun for self-defence," he replied.

Oscar shook his head. "What about my editor?" he asked, exaggerated. "He understands the interests that article will create; doesn't he require a weapon?"

"It'll be too late for the Titans to stop your editor. But they think that you're running the show. Obviously, it means that they will try to stop you."

"I really hope that you're right because he only has my antique letter opener to fend with," Oscar said smiling.

CHAPTER 15

*"**WE** HAVE A news special that General Burgoyne, one of the most respectable Generals in the British Army has been assassinated in his holiday home in Greece."*

It was a Friday evening and his television was on. Oscar was resting upon his sofa. He wondered if the Titans were responsible for his death and why? Brooks continued to think about having an early night but his football team, Fulham, was playing in a cup tournament. The programme would reveal if his team, the underdogs, were triumphant. The coverage on General Burgoyne was making a lot of speculations on the killers: Communist sympathizers; Neo-Nazis; Greek patriots, and the criminal underworld. Oscar was nodding off to sleep but his phone rang.

"Oscar here," he acknowledged.

"Oscar, we need to meet up straight away."

"Who is this?"

"Graham," he replied.

"What do you want?"

"It's about the Titans, why else would I call you? Meet me at the Windsor car park. I will be near a blue trailer on the right. Now!" he said and hung-up.

Oscar sat in his seat to evaluate that call. He also looked at the time on his watch and the news would finish within 5 minutes. So he waited patiently for a sports presenter to deliver it. There wasn't a result as it would be shown on a special football programme afterwards. Oscar decided that it would be best to buy tomorrow's paper and so got himself ready to go out. Dressing casually, he jumped into his car.

***

A car barrier prevented him gaining access onto the site that he parked his car along the street. As Oscar got out, he observed that the street lights were poorly lit and there wasn't a whisper. Nevertheless, he lost his balance after a cold gust of wind passed by. He then stood to face the car park itself. It looked badly kept: weed spots could have been seen growing through the tarmac;

potholes were discovered every twenty yards in all directions; it was also poorly lit and there wasn't much of security. It was an abandoned car park yet several cars seemed to dare use it. Oscar wondered how those cars got in and he walked a while along the perimeter: several parts of the wall had crumbled. Anyway, Oscar walked onto the site and saw an old blue trailer to his right.

"Am here!" he said as he was approaching.

Goddammit, I should have I bought my gun, he thought as he got nearer to it. The trailer door opened. Oscar stopped to see who would be coming out. Nobody revealed themselves to him.

"This is Oscar. Show yourself now!"

No response from within. Brooks stood his ground. "Look here, if you wanted to see me in person, show yourself. Otherwise, I'll be turning back you arsehole!" he said defiant.

Still there wasn't a reply.

Oscar turned about but heard foot-steps behind him. He spun around. A man was in front of him and couldn't be seen properly as he stood in the shadows. Oscar could see another man just peeping out of the trailer too.

"Oscar isn't it?"

"Is that you?"

"Who were you expecting to see?" the man now asked.

"I asked first!" Oscar told him.

"I asked second, yes. But mine is more relevant."

"Graham, this isn't funny, you expected me to come here. So what do you want to talk about?"

"I'm not Graham," he replied.

"Are you part of God's Angels?" Oscar asked.

The man smirked. "Am I Graham? No I'm not Graham nor am I part of that pathetic movement. Have you forgotten already who this is?"

"I don't have time for this. Besides, I'll decide on whom I ought to meet up with," Oscar said and made his way to exit the premise.

"Not so fast boy!"

Oscar turned around again, he shouted, "Listen here you cheeky bastard!" He continued, showing him his fist, "I have better things to do than spending time listening to you!"

"No you do not and you'll never!" the man remarked as he got closer.

Oscar was walking backwards. "So where is Graham?"

"He's inside the trailer," he responded. "Don't you want to see him?"

Oscar stopped. "What is he doing?"

"I think he's waiting for you, son," the dark figure now replied and was still getting nearer.

"Just stop there!" Oscar shouted. "Bring him out now!"

"No can do as he's asleep in the trailer," the man responded.

Oscar gasped in recognition as he continued to advance on him. "It's you!"

Max laughed. "This is just so easy," he said and was pointing his gun at him.

"So what are you doing here?" Oscar asked, shocked too.

"So you're a dare devil by asking the master to subdue, isn't it?"

"You're the one with the gun," Oscar implied.

"That's very true indeed for I'm here to meet you again," Max said.

"What did you do to Graham?"

"Nothing that I'll do to you," he replied.

Oscar froze but Max alluded on where he ought to go. All he could do was oblige to his demand. Nothing was making any sense why Graham wanted to meet him. Again, how did the Titans know he was going to see him? Despite Oscar being perplexed, he took a step inside. There was something disturbing when he entered the room as the curtains hadn't been cleaned and the smell it seem to produce filled the air; an odour. Besides that, the blue carpet was poorly kept; mud marks were seen everywhere and fluff too. The only pieces of furniture were a large table and fold-up chairs. The table was placed near the far-side and the chairs stacked upon one another near the door. Another person was waiting inside and he was pointing his gun at him.

"So we meet again, Oscar," the man said.

Oscar didn't reply as he was getting tied up from behind and his mouth stuffed with a silk hanky. Also, Max made him lie upon the floor.

"It's nice to meet you," he repeated, "once more." He moved closer to Oscar and knelt over him. "I always ask myself why you take the trouble of daring yourself. Look at you, tied up and I have the power to end your life."

Oscar was trying to speak his mind but being gagged prevented him.

"I understand that you feel important to your paper but the truth hurts. People are going to die tonight."

Still Oscar was struggling to speak and was moving along the floor like a worm.

The man laughed. "Stop squealing," he continued, "it's no use fighting fate. You have been a pain in the arse. Snooping around where you're not wanted; you were trying to expose our objectives. This will all end now."

Max laughed too as he pulled out a huge needle from his inside pocket. "This can knock out an elephant!" He moved towards Oscar and jabbed him in his arm.

***

Oscar's head was swimming as he got up — he instantly remembered Windsor. Trying to adjust to the light, he rubbed his eyes but felt them getting worse. Oscar rubbed harder to no avail that he used his sleeve to dry them. When he came to, his hands were covered in blood. Oscar was also in a room that he had never been before; it was very stylish for a kitchen and he approached the sink to wash his hands. It struck him that the blood wasn't his; he flitted out of the room to see whose it was. He flipped a switch and stood in the lounge: no clue. That house only had one floor and as he went into the next room, Oscar saw a body, face down and motionless. Oscar knew who it was—

"Oh my God! No!"

There was a pool of blood when he turned the dead body around. He couldn't understand why he was alive and looked around to see if Graham was there: He wasn't. He saw a telephone along the hallway and picked it up to dial for the police.

"I want the—"

He hung up. Something just didn't add up why he was still alive? Why was there a dead body lying on the carpet? Oscar thought that he must leave the crime scene. He found a coat before opening the front door onto the street. Oscar hadn't any money on him and didn't know where he actually was. He had to speak to Amanda. He had to speak to God's Angels on how to tackle his dilemma. He had to find Graham as well. Oscar saw a couple heading his way.

"Excuse me," he said, "Where am I?"

"This is Bovil Street."

"Ah! This is in Hammersmith, right?"

"Of course."

That couple carried on their own business as Oscar made his exit. However, He didn't know what he was doing that he retreated back into the flat.

He picked up the telephone. "I want the police at 14 Bovil Street in Hammersmith. There has been a murder."

Oscar waited in the flat for two minutes. He pondered on how he was going to explain about the victim: His version wouldn't stick. He searched around to find some money and a mobile. He left the apartment again and ran down the street onto a junction. He flagged a taxi and jumped inside.

"Can you take me to...Wait...I just got to make a call!"

He dialled and it rang a short time.

"Amanda we need to talk about Graham, fast. Where can I meet you?"

"I suppose the Roxy nightclub."

***

Oscar walked into the club and saw Amanda waiting at the counter; it was a quiet night as he approached her.

"What were you saying about Graham?"

Oscar sat on the stool beside her. "I was supposed to meet up with Graham but we got jumped: It was them."

Amanda asked, "Where were you meeting him?"

"Windsor car park but the thing is that I got jumped by those Titans. I woke up half an hour ago covered in blood which belonged to my editor's: He's bloody dead!"

Amanda looked around before comforting him. "Take it easy. This is quite a serious situation. You were saying that you were covered in blood?"

Oscar only nodded.

"They are trying to frame you for his murder. Do you know how he was killed?"

"I saw blood, I guess it's a gunshot wound."

"Are you positively sure? Did you find the gun there?" Amanda asked.

"There was no gun that I could see."

"Did you check the house?"

"I checked certain things," he replied.

"Oscar, you're fucked up," she said. "Does anybody else know about the murder?"

"I've informed the police."

"It'll be routine to treat you as a suspect. I don't know what to say to you," Amanda said.

"I want to know what has happened to Graham. Is he loose?" Oscar asked.

Amanda searched into her jacket pocket for her mobile. She had no answer and placed it back. She shook her head too. "He's not answering."

"We should go to the Windsor car park now. Maybe he's there," he said.

"We can take my car there," she said. "You should consider changing your clothes soon: You will be considered the main suspect."

"Let's go to my place. I've a gun there that—"

"I'm carrying one, don't worry," she insisted.

They both left the bar and walked to the back of the club. It was starting to rain as she entered into her blue Fiesta. "Where is that Windsor car park?" Amanda asked.

"If I remember correctly, it's actually along the outskirts of Earling."

Amanda resorted to use her smartphone. "Here it is and it's not too far from here," she said before starting up her engine.

***

"I never knew that you carried a gun," Oscar said.

"Yeah, Antonis gave me this after my dad got arrested. You can never tell who you can trust," Amanda replied.

"What do you mean?"

"It's just on how on earth the Titans knew about the planned publication. We didn't tell them anything."

"Tagging phones, isn't it?"

"Basically, we could easily be dealing with the secret service. We are considered a threat and for what?" Amanda wondered to herself.

"Turn left here," Oscar said after he recognised the dilapidated site and his own car.

She drove through a breached wall and Oscar could see the trailer ahead of him. He was pointing at it and Amanda stopped short. She went into her glove compartment to retrieve her gun.

"You do know how to use that?" Oscar asked.

"What! I just point the gun at the target and pull the trigger. It's not that hard, boy," she replied and took the safety off it.

They both got out of the car and Amanda left her head-lights on. Oscar was surprised on how Amanda was conducting herself; she was telling him to move out of the beam to flank the trailer. It was exactly what he was trained to do in his urban training with the SAS. They both crept towards the trailer looking to see if anybody would come out. It did seem that they were the only people there that Amanda tried to open the door. It was locked. Amanda was still cautious as she moved to the rear to see anyone lurking about. She saw an opened window and silently moved towards it—

Bang! Amanda heard the front door being smashed through and she made haste to Oscar—

"What do you think you are doing?"

"I figured that the rear was secure so I kicked the door in," he responded.

"Next time you're thinking to pull that kind of stunt, tell me first," she said.

Anyway, they both entered the trailer and Amanda turned on the light switch. As the room lightened up, they saw Graham lying on the floor tied up. Oscar approached and freed him.

"What has just happened?" Graham asked.

"We were visited by the Titans," Oscar responded.

Graham got to his feet. "So who freed you?"

"They set me free at a crime scene."

"What do you mean?"

"My editor is murdered."

"So if I'm thinking correctly, you'll the main suspect that the police will be looking for?"

"We don't have much time," Amanda said. "We still need to get that list."

Graham asked, "She's right. We really need to get that list, Oscar. So you were saying that your dead editor had the list?"

"I've now got it," Oscar admitted

"Is it on you?"

"I've left it in my apartment."

Amanda was pointing her gun at Oscar. "Wait just a minute," she said, "I thought you woke up at the crime scene and went straight to Roxy's?"

"OK, I had it all along," he admitted again.

Graham tapped Amanda on the shoulder. "If you don't mind, can you place that gun out of harm's way?" he asked.

Amanda placed it near Graham on a table. "Why are you so nervous?"

"We need him alive to get that list," he replied.

Oscar shook his head. "So that's why I'm not a member of your pathetic cult? It's all because I'm not good enough."

Amanda frowned at him. "Just what are you talking about?" she asked.

He wouldn't answer her but raised his hands in the air. Amanda was perplexed by his actions and turned around. They both could see that Graham was pointing her gun at them.

"Well, this is delightful, isn't it?" Graham said.

Amanda was shocked to find herself raising her hands too. "What are you doing?"

"I'm doing what is right," he replied.

"You're one of them aren't you? You meeting me here was part of your little elaborate game, isn't it?" Oscar asked.

He smiled and laughed heavily. "You are a clever man, aren't you? So it has taken you all of this time to figure that one out?"

"Antonis trusted you!" Amanda said.

"Yes that's true but things can change. I was his lieutenant — in the most part — but you just have to accept the beauty of the Titans," Graham reacted.

"So when did you turn coat?" Amanda now asked.

"It was just before your father was going to have his little celebration with those dead people. The truth is that the Titans do offer a better world. It's one where we eliminate wars and strife. It's a world that your father failed to grasp," he replied.

"No they offered you money," Oscar concluded.

Graham laughed a lot louder. "You do catch on well. Money is the objective here and the Titans have a net worth over billions of pounds."

"Doing what?"

"We do researches for a better tomorrow," he now replied.

"So what is going to happen to us?" Amanda asked.

Graham stopped laughing. "Unfortunately, the pair of you will be dead by this very gun."

"Just wait a moment," Oscar said in his calm tone.

Graham looked congenial. "Are you asking me that you want to live a few seconds more? Just what the hell are you talking about?"

"You're forgetting Clive Roberts. He'll hear about this and his views will look more compelling," Oscar responded.

"You really think that Titans are naïve? Of course, Clive is already being dealt with. Just as we're speaking now, my superiors will be making arrangements for him to be on the news again: He's going to take his own life," he said.

Amanda looked to her feet in shame. "How deep are you in that group?" she asked.

"I'm deep enough."

"Just hear us out," Oscar said and was trying to move towards him.

"Now you just hold it there," Graham said as his trigger finger was firmly on him. "I'll kill you."

"Yes you will but before we go, there's something that you really ought to know," Oscar said as he stepped back and moved away from Amanda.

"I can see what you're doing," Graham said. "You think that I'm stupid don't you? I focus my gun on you while Amanda is out of my line of fire."

"But Amanda is over there," he said without making a sudden movement. "There is one thing that I think you ought to know before you leave this god forsaken place."

"There's nothing that you can say that will change this situation," Graham stated.

"But," Oscar went on, "you really think Amanda, in the first place, approached a journalist and informed him to *defeat the dark world*?"

Graham was suddenly thinking about it and at that spilt second, Oscar jerked to the left that the gun discharged. Oscar knew that time was the essence as he dodged the bullet. He held his arm high that Graham fired yet again into the ceiling. Speckle of dust fell upon his eyes that Oscar had enough time to grab the gun along its barrel. The gun fired the third time before Oscar was now able to strike him across his face. Graham fell upon one of his knees, and was pulling out something from behind. Oscar had to stop him. He stuck him across the head with his repossessed gun that Graham fell flat on his back.

"Just stop right there, Graham," he said.

Graham sat up, in a daze, staring at the pair. "I had my orders to annihilate you. This won't be easy."

"So you grassed up my father?" Amanda asked him.

"I only know certain things on what the Titans are planning to accomplish," he replied.

"Turn face down on your front!" Oscar ordered him.

"What's the point? You'll both die soon enough. We have agents everywhere. Your father is going to die and there's nothing that you can do to change that."

"I said turn around!" Oscar shouted again.

"Why do you think that you can murder me?"

"Boy, you have no idea what I'm capable of," Oscar replied.

"You are just a journalist for a small newspaper in the city. God knows how you managed to escape Greece. I slipped up." Graham continued, "A moment ago you were saying that the dark world wasn't brought to you by Amanda, right?"

"I've figured that you were only interested in the list not my source," Oscar responded.

"May I ask who it is?"

"An old friend of mine," he answered.

"Who was it?"

"Why is that important?" Oscar now asked.

"Because I wouldn't be sitting on my arse," he reacted.

Amanda approached Oscar for her gun. "Give that to me and disarm him."

Oscar responded, "Not after he turns onto his front."

"Listen here soldier-boy, that's mine gun!"

"And he's dangerous," Oscar responded.

"Let me see what's behind him then," she said.

"Not until he turns around, Amanda!" he shouted.

"Graham," she said to him, "he'll kill you if you don't turn around."

He laughed. "A journalist killing me? That's nonsense."

"You've no idea what kind of person I was," Oscar reacted.

"Well, will you enlighten me?"

"SAS."

"So that explains how you can manage to get out of difficult situations, yes?"

"Now turn around," Oscar requested.

"OK," Graham said, "you win but there is still time to save your father, Amanda."

"Don't listen to him," Oscar said. "He's trying to manipulate the situation!"

Amanda said to Graham, "I now know that you idolise your masters so why should I believe you?"

"Do you really have a choice?"

"Give me my gun back," she asked Oscar.

"Not until he's faced down on the floor."

Graham turned to his front in a quick fashion before deciding to roll under the table: out of their sight!

"Move back!" Oscar ordered and signalled at Amanda.

A fourth bullet was at play which narrowly passed Amanda as she moved. Oscar quickly jumped upon the wooden table that created its sound — he had to leap off in a new direction. As he landed, he saw that Graham was looking at him and shooting at the table.

"You cheeky bastard!" Oscar said and fired his gun.

Graham checked his stomach and saw blood pouring out of him. He lifted his gun—

Bang!

Amanda wasn't sure who was shooting whom. "Oscar, speak to me?"

"He's dead," he replied after taking his concealed weapon.

She approached the table and saw two fatal wounds. "What did he mean that my father is going to die?"

"He was toying with us," he said.

"So how do you know?"

"He was showing off," Oscar now replied.

"But I believed him. It seems that my father is able to expose them in prison. They will kill him."

"Why is it now but not before?"

"Perhaps to give him a demeanour first, that he's a brutal murderer which no one will care about," Amanda conjectured. "We're so fucked."

Amanda was pacing around. "We need to return to Roxy."

"What's there?"

"I kinda own the nightclub and I also have an apartment above it," Amanda said.

Oscar felt confused. "But I stopped at your place in Chelsea?"

"That's my primary home," she replied.

"So why are we going to Roxy?"

"Just shut up and follow me!"

The pair left the trailer and headed towards her car. It was still a quiet night as she drove back to the club. There was hardly any traffic on the road and the streets were relatively empty. At some point, Oscar had to raise his concerns. "Amanda, just what exactly are God's Angels?"

"We're the opposite from those Titans. We serve to expose them to the world."

"Cost a lot of lives along the way. So what were you doing with that gun if it isn't for home defence?"

"You never noticed the danger element?"

"OK," he conceded. "I'll have to attend with the police and answer their enquiries."

"They mustn't attempt to ask you anything because you'll be arrested and be charged for your editor's murder," Amanda responded.

"I was a journalist yesterday. Now I'm a wanted fugitive."

"So we need to somehow warn my father about the imminent danger. Also where is that list really?"

"It's at my apartment."

She stopped her car. "Sometimes, you don't make any sense when you answer me. I thought you said that you weren't covering the story?"

"That's the truth," he said. "Oh my God, Lucy!"

"Who's that?"

"She could be in danger because the Titans must have been beating information out of Stuart!"

"Oscar, we haven't the time—"

Oscar interrupted, "We must make time! This is my fault entirely; I was trying to make Stuart look big!"

CHAPTER 16

LUCY WAS IN bed when she heard her doorbell ringing early that morning. She was dreaming of bright blue skies; a mild summer breeze and windmills that she tried to clasp onto them. The doorbell rang again. Lucy held the pillow over her head. However, she could still hear that noise and her dream was now lost.

"Just who the hell wants to wake me up?" she whispered to herself.

Lucy turned to her boyfriend who seemed to be sleeping sound. She put on her dressing gown and slippers to head to the front door. Behind it she asked. "Who's that?"

"It's me, Oscar."

"What do you want?"

"Will you let us in?"

"What do you mean by *us*?" Lucy asked.

"I've a friend here."

Lucy opened the door acutely. "This better be good," she said.

"Will you let us in?"

She was reluctant but opened it wider and pointed to her visitors to sit in her lounge.

"It's about Stuart," Oscar said.

Lucy was half-asleep as she yawned. "So he's managed to fire you?"

"It's not that. He's murdered."

She joined her guests on the sofa. "What do you mean he's murdered?"

"Lucy," Oscar continued, "you noticed that Bentley and those horrific incidents in Greece? It's all interconnected."

Lucy shook her head. "The report that I was going to do, and that notepad—"

"You mustn't try to see to the story getting published. We must scrap it," Oscar said.

"So you want to do the story instead?" Lucy asked.

"It's likely that I've been framed for his murder. I won't be able to go to work at all. I won't even be able to go home as well," he said.

"So you came here to warn me that somebody will kill me if I go ahead with the story?"

"I'm saying that the Titans may have you on their minds."

"Why do you say that?"

"It's because they had—"

"Who's that, darling," said the voice from upstairs.

"It's nothing dear. Just go back to bed. It's just about work," Lucy responded.

Oscar resumed, "They took him out and I'm sure that they'd questioned him on what he knows about them."

"What makes you think that they interrogated him?"

Oscar looked at Amanda who was looking away. He faced Lucy. "It has been a long night. I don't know what they know."

"Oscar. You're getting just a little too paranoid for my liking," Lucy said. "But you say Stuart is dead?"

Amanda nodded. "He's right, they've got to him. It's highly likely that Oscar has been framed for his murder."

"So who are you?" Lucy asked.

Oscar answered, "She's Clive Roberts' daughter."

"If you're in trouble with the law, what are you doing here?"

"I don't know," he said. "I just thought that you'll be in danger."

"I think you better leave," Lucy said and got up to head to the front door.

"Please Lucy, you mustn't do the story. Or you will be dead!"

"Will you stop shouting as my boyfriend is upstairs," she whispered.

"Don't you get it? The Bentley; the shootout at the resort; the car chase—"

"So I don't mention the list and what about Don McQueen? He may order me to do the front page."

"Out of a respect for Stuart," Oscar replied. "Just say that you cannot do the story."

227

"Are you going to hand yourself in to the police?" Lucy now asked — still half-awake.

He shook his head. "I'm in this shit too deep. I just got to find out what the Titans are actually doing,"

"I'll tell the police that you were here — when prompted."

Amanda responded, "So you'll tell them that I was here?"

Lucy thought for a moment. "Why do you expect me to lie?"

"Lucy, you do understand that there's a dark force at play. Please don't squeal on her."

"OK, I just say that I wasn't fully awake when you came banging on my door. You better go."

The pair left Lucy's home. There wasn't a farewell as she closed the door behind them. A fox was spotted a distance away. It was staring at them as they approached her car and it wandered off into the night.

They sat in the vehicle. It was quiet so Amanda decided to put on the radio. A love song was being played but turned it off. She said, "I'll need to inform Antonis about this fuck-up: My father is in trouble."

"What about me? I'll be considered a murderer."

"I'm talking about somebody's life," she said then grabbed her mobile from her pocket...There wasn't a response.

Still in the stationary car, Amanda said, "I don't know how to stop them killing my father."

"Those bastards think that they can get away with anything. One thing is for certain: They aren't invincible," Oscar said.

Amanda decided to turn on her ignition and pulled out onto the road, she headed towards a T-junction to turn left.

"Wait a minute," Oscar said.

"What you've a plan for my father's safety?"

"Look into your rear-view mirror. I can see a Bentley parking outside Lucy's," he said.

She spotted the car turning off its headlights. "What of it?"

"I've been followed around by a Bentley recently. They are here for Lucy."

Amanda didn't know what to do but Oscar signalled her to make a turn onto the main road to halt her car. "I'll have to sneak up to evaluate the situation."

Amanda reacted, "You may have been in the SAS, but it doesn't mean I cannot sneak—"

"Just keep a low profile," he intervened, "and everything will be fine."

The pair climbed out of the car and crept towards the corner of the street. Oscar gave a hand sign for her to stop behind him as he took a peek. Brooks could only make little sense on his observation. There weren't many residential street lights and a lot of cars were parked along it. He pressed on forward.

"What about me?" Amanda asked.

"Just wait there," he responded.

Of course, the street itself was full of parked cars that he went behind the first. He moved onto the next to get a better view. He didn't have a vantage point and moved along several more cars. He made another peep and a hand grasped his shoulder. He turned, in a sudden, in anticipation that Max was going to kill him, but it was Amanda.

"I told you to wait," he whispered.

"Look here, I don't draw attention," she said.

"Just wait right here," he told her again and headed on to find a better place to locate the car. Brooks saw a large gap between two cars which gave him a better view across the street. They were people sitting in one of the cars. It seemed to Oscar that they were spooked since Amanda didn't take her turn when there wasn't any incoming traffic. Oscar pulled out his gun and was to determine his next move. Brooks couldn't identify them; he waited. The people were now moving inside. Oscar didn't have a clear shot on them — he daren't make an awful scene. One of them got out and was looking in all directions. Oscar had to break his view by hiding behind the car wheel. He timed to move into a better position to see what was going to happen. The man approached Lucy's front door and began ringing on the bell. Again, Oscar timed his move pass the car space behind another. He made a dash to the other side of the road. He waited again. Oscar took another glimpse and the man was still waiting outside.

"She must be fast sleep," Max said as he approached his car.

"Keep trying, we got until sunlight."

"If that is the case, she better have that list," Max implied.

Oscar could see him heading back to the front door and was pressing on the doorbell.

"Now you fucking listen," Lucy said after looking through her bedroom window, "I don't know what game you think that you're playing at, but it's early in the darn morning!"

"I'm extremely sorry," Max responded and pulled out his identity card, "we're working for the MI6. It's about national security. Will you let us come in?"

"I don't care if you take the Queen's corgis for a walk!" she shouted and closed the window.

"Perhaps another time." Max repeated, "Perhaps another time."

Oscar was alarmed that that man worked for secret service. He was flabbergasted that the Titans were involved with Greek drug-lords too. And was stupefied on what Amanda's father was trying to reveal.

The car sped off and it turned at the junction. Amanda was walking-up-straight towards Lucy's. "Where are you Oscar," she said.

"Amanda, get yourself down!" Oscar shouted.

She dropped behind a car thinking that she had mistaken the wrong Bentley. She could hear foot-steps getting closer to her position that she dashed onto the other side of the street to duck.

Max shouted, "If I'm drunk than you're here Oscar, isn't it?"

Oscar made no reply.

"Let me tell you this," Max carried on saying, "that you do make a terrible undercover reporter: You parked that car at the top of the junction and that's the teller if you were wondering."

Oscar remained silent.

"You can tell that bitch that we'll make another call during the day. Or do us all a favour and hand over that list."

"What makes you think that she has the list?" Oscar asked aloud.

Max pulled out his gun and headed towards his location. "Because why are you here?"

"She's a decoy! I know about Graham," Oscar added.

"What? That he was helping us?"

"He told me everything," Oscar confirmed.

Max laughed. "That he wanted to rise to the top? We just want that list."

"Don't make another move or I will be provoked to take necessary steps," Oscar warned.

Max stood still behind a car. "Give us the list and I'll pretend that nothing has happened tonight."

"If I gave you the list, you'll harm her."

"Not at all. Trust me since no harm was placed on Amanda's father," Max said.

"But you're planning to sort out loose ends, isn't it?"

"I cannot deny that but you can still save your friends," Max returned.

Oscar could see Amanda pointing from behind a car. He made a peek but turned away as the gunman fired. Since Max had had a silencer, Oscar could hear the ricochet behind his cover. Oscar shot his weapon into that direction which made a loud sound. A few residential lights were being turned on as he fired again.

"We'll meet again soon," Max said before he made himself scarce.

Oscar stayed put for a moment as the neighbourhood was becoming alive. He ran towards Amanda. "We'll have to leave this place."

She concurred and they hastily headed straight to her car.

"They're MI6 agents," Oscar said.

"What makes you think that?"

"It's what they told Lucy," he replied.

Amanda pulled out onto the road. "This is getting worse. Now they will know that this car belonged to me."

"They do know that you're Clive's daughter, right?"

"What a dumb thing to ask. Of course! My father always told me that it's best to keep a low profile to stay alive. Now they'll know that I was here with you."

"They didn't see you. In any case, just report that the car was stolen," Oscar said, paranoid too.

"You're too sure of yourself that those men understand reason."

"Have you phoned Antonis?"

"Of course, but he isn't answering his phone."

"It looks like you'll need to be in hiding with me," Oscar suggested.

She wouldn't answer him.

"Do you know any good places where we can kip?"

"Roxy's," she replied. "The club and the premise are under my pseudonym name."

Oscar smiled. "Silly me —of course— we really do need to ditch this car," he recommended.

CHAPTER 17

ON THE FOLLOWING day, Amanda was going to meet up with Antonis at a new shopping mall. Oscar was wearing a cap and sunglasses to attend there too (She bought him a new pair of trousers, jumper and a bomber jacket). It was very busy and she was to find him at a fast food restaurant. Just to walk in wasn't plain sailing as many families were waiting in the queue and a lot of seats were taken. Amanda was five minutes late and both she and Oscar went on every floor to find him. He was found sitting alone with a soft drink beckoning them over.

"Please join me," Antonis said.

"Thanks Antonis, this is—"

"I know who you are," he interjected, "the one that wouldn't give-up his list. So why are you here?"

Amanda took a deep breath. "It's Graham: he's the mole."

Antonis looked placid on the revelation. "How can you tell?"

"It's because he was threatening to kill us," Oscar responded.

"Where is he now?"

"I've killed him last night at a dilapidated site. He confessed that he was Titans. We also had a run with other agents trying to find that list."

"So you do have it?"

Oscar nodded. "It's actually in my possession."

Antonis nodded. "So I must take that list and use it for good use. It has been difficult enough to physically speak to Clive Roberts," he said.

Amanda added, "They are now planning to kill my father."

"Who told you—"

"Graham was boasting about it as he was trying to kill us," she said. "Also, he did plea about it for his own life."

"Your father," Antonis continued, "is a brave man who believes in our cause. Without him, I would have had nothing to give to this fight."

Amanda asked, "Why did you trust Graham?"

Antonis sucked on his straw before answering. "He was employed at the British Embassy by your father." He carried on saying, "In fact, Graham convinced him to join our cause. There's a negative presence in Greece which is unmistakable."

"What is that supposed to mean?" Oscar asked.

"Since I was a child in Greece, I saw many terrible things: The regime, the student killings and drug pushing. Yet, something is much more horrific at play in my country. I only heard it as a rumour but it's getting louder after Clive Roberts confessed it to me."

"What did he confess?" Amanda asked.

"The British government is involved in drug-trafficking in my beloved country."

Oscar was perplexed. "I could understand the criminal element but I cannot make sense why our British government is involved in that."

"He wanted to tell me more but he feared that such information mustn't be taken on lightly. That's why he thought to publish his diary. The whole procedure to print was supposed to be hush-hush but somehow they knew," he said.

"That's because that bastard, Graham, snitched on him," Amanda said.

"So it might seem," Antonis agreed.

"Wait here," Oscar said. "Are you expecting more moles in your movement?"

"I've learnt to expect the worse," he answered.

"So you're now thinking," Oscar went on, "that Amanda and I are not worthy to be your allies?"

Antonis took another sip from his straw. "This is a very good mango flavoured drink. You should try some, yes?"

"Don't you trust us?"

"My father," Amanda said, "told me never to trust anybody in our movement."

Oscar was getting irritated. "Don't you trust me?"

"Look here young man," Antonis said, "I heard that you were in the SAS, right?"

He nodded.

"Why did you trust those soldiers?"

"We were like brothers. We trust each other because we are the best on what we do."

Antonis hummed. "That's very good as a SAS man so you follow orders, yes?"

Oscar responded, "Of course we follow orders."

"To the letter, isn't it?"

Oscar nodded.

"So what could possibly be wrong with the Titans; a group that imposes orders on others? So there isn't anything wrong with that?"

"In the SAS, we were serving for our majesty. That was the job," Oscar replied.

"You served for the British government and we believe that powerful Titan agents had infiltrated it. I even the Ministry of Defence."

"So you think that a SAS soldier was trying to beat me up; shoot me dead and run me off the road? You fear that I'll go rogue?"

Antonis drank some more of his soft drink. "You mustn't assume the obvious if you don't understand the latent," he replied.

"Anyway," Oscar said, "it's very likely that I'm a wanted fugitive for the murder of my former employer. I've been framed by them."

"It's true," Amanda concurred. "He woke up in the victim's blood."

"Sounds like you had a very long night, isn't it," Antonis said.

"All I want to do now is get to the bottom of that group. They have messed up my career, my life and they have murdered an innocent man," Oscar stated.

Antonis didn't show much of a change in his composure. "If you were in my shoes, what do you make of Graham who told me something similar to what I'm hearing now? He was just as energetic to thrash them."

"I suppose that you'll just have to trust me," he responded.

"Which I will but don't expect me to see you as trustworthy any time soon," Antonis said.

"He saved my life last night," Amanda informed.

Antonis nodded. "You may join us in our cause. It was a mistake on giving Graham a lot of responsibilities that he just cracked. I've should have seen that coming."

Oscar asked, "What do you mean that I can join your cause? I was already part of your cause, wasn't I?"

Antonis laughed a bit. "Then everybody here is more than welcomed to join us, yes?"

"So what's our next move?" Amanda asked her leader.

"Well, it seems that the list is a highly-valued acquisition. You do have the list?"

Amanda looked straight at Oscar. He had a qualm and was scratching his head. "I don't actually have it."

Antonis frowned on his news. "So I'll be making another mistake on a man that doesn't take our movement seriously. If I understand it, you've been told about God's Angels, isn't it?"

Oscar gave a verbal nod.

"You wouldn't pass on the list to Graham, why?"

"Because it could make a difference between life and death," he answered.

"And now you don't have it, isn't it?"

"It's in a safe place, I can assure you," he now replied.

"All bets will be off if you fail to deliver that list to me. Do you understand?" Antonis asked.

"What bets?" Oscar now asked perplexed as well.

"If you're on the run, I can help you on that," Antonis responded.

"You can?"

"He can," Amanda reinstated to him.

Antonis continued, "If you don't mind—"

"No wait," Oscar interrupted, "you're treating this damn to casual for my liking. Graham gave you up to the Titans. They're looking for you as well."

Antonis was just about to stand but he stayed seated. "That's very true. They could be lurking around in this shopping mall and monitoring my every move," he said. "I dare say that you're more of a dangerous threat than I am."

"So I've killed a few men," he confirmed, sarcastic too.

"We've never ever killed anybody but you have done," Antonis said. "You'll be a prime target."

"But Graham gave you up," Oscar said.

"So my name is Antonis and I look a certain way, yes?"

"You'd have been profiled, isn't it?"

"Hmm," he carried on, "so what do you recommend that I should do?"

"Well, hide."

"That's exactly what I'm going to do," he said.

Antonis rose from his seat drinking his soft drink. "Remember that I can help you get out of your predicament if you bring that list to me."

Oscar watched him as he made his exit. "He's rather relaxed, isn't he?"

"He's always like that. Even if we'd severed the head of the snake, he just reacts as if it wasn't significant," Amanda replied.

"Why is he the leader?" Oscar asked. "He has obviously failed to pick a better lieutenant."

"It was his movement that converted my father. It was his movement that made my father believe that he was wrong but to follow the righteous path ahead."

"And what was that?"

"Just to be frank: Accept Christ as our Lord."

Oscar laughed out loud. "Wait, are you telling me that you're some kind of exorcist?"

"Antonis was right about you."

Oscar composed himself. "He's some kind of reverend?"

"Let me tell you a story about Antonis. He ran a bible study class in Greece who welcomed my father to his fellowship. They talked about God's plan on making our world a better place to live in. One time, Antonis discussed about his country's national holiday on November 17th. It was the day when students stood up against tyranny. My father broke down and told him about that secret group planning to undermine his people. Antonis forgave him and offered him refuge.

"Antonis told him to go public about what he knows of the Titans. But as you know, he got stitched up."

"It sounds pretty noble of him. Yet, just how did Graham became his lieutenant?"

"It was Graham who introduced Clive to the Bible classes. Antonis saw a man who was determined to bring out the good in people," Amanda said.

"Antonis thinks that I could become a *bad guy*, doesn't he?"

Amanda wouldn't answer as she was looking over his shoulder. Oscar was about to turn around—

"Look at me, Oscar. Do not draw any attention," Amanda said.

Oscar raised an eyebrow. "What's going on behind me?"

"The editor's death is now news. I can only imagine what he's reading," she replied.

"I think that we should go," Oscar said as he got up.

They both made their way out of the mall to the car park at the back of it — adjacent to the building. Amanda climbed into her car with him.

"I was trying to tell you back there that Antonis thinks that I might turn dirty. Do you agree?"

"If that's the case, I'll just have to kill you," Amanda remarked.

"So how is he going to save your father?" Oscar now asked her.

"I don't know. He didn't say," Amanda answered.

"Let me get this straight, your cult leader is taking on a vicious organisation by offering them a peace token?"

"You don't seem bothered on making obnoxious jokes, don't you? So again, why should Antonis trust you?"

"It has been a long night. I did work for the London Eagle just before I got pulled up to meet Graham. I've lost everything and Lucy probably thinks that I've killed Stuart (I'm trying to make light of a pretty awful situation!). God, you make it sound that one day, I just gonna give you all up to the Titans — after all that I've been through."

"We need that list," Amanda hinted.

"But you do trust me?"

"As long as you aren't out of my sight," she said. "We still need that list."

"Let's go and get it," Oscar said.

Amanda wouldn't turn on her engine. She just stared at him. "In the shopping mall that man was reading his newspaper about you. Your place will be swarmed by the police. You cannot possibly think that you can just walk through the front door with a big smile on your face?" she asked, of course, being satiric.

"I wasn't thinking—"

"You weren't thinking at all. I'm stuck with you without Antonis' full blessing. Do you not understand the risks that I'll be taking for you? The police will be all-over London," she said. "Oh," she went on, "what about your colleagues trying to track your last movements?"

"I wasn't thinking—"

"No you weren't thinking at all, damn you!" she now said. "Without that list we'll have no option but to go to Greece to that Consul-General. A dangerous job where Titans are trying to kill us? Wait! How are you going to Greece if we won't be able to create a fraudulent passport?"

247

"Amanda will you just listen," he said. "I wasn't thinking about that as I can enter from the back!"

CHAPTER 18

IT WAS GETTING late when Amanda parked her car some distance from Oscar's apartment. During the day, it was sunny and hot. Nevertheless, it was still very warm. Amanda's car was fairly humid — even with the windows winded down. She fancied walking around the empty streets as the cool breeze and the moonlight were her evening welcoming. Unfortunately, her passenger was her main concern.

"Here we are," Amanda said.

Oscar looked at her and smiled. "This should be easy peasy lemon squeezy," he said.

"Nobody says that anymore."

"I still do."

"You might as well enter through the front, provided the police aren't on patrol for you," Amanda said.

"That's hardly likely."

"So let me take a look."

Oscar inclined and she got out of her car. Amanda only walked a short distance that she returned.

"What is it?" Oscar asked.

"It would help if you tell me exactly where you lived?"

"You know, Good Mews and it is number 135. It's on the second floor," Oscar advised. "Oh one more thing," he continued, "You'll need to take my keys to get into the apartment building." He indicated which key it was. "There will be a lot of CCTV around the premises so wear my cap," he said.

Amanda took his cap. "Why didn't you tell me that before?"

"I'm sorry, but I was just thinking about the rear security," he answered.

"You worry about that afterwards."

She pressed on towards the apartments along the main road. A few were staring at her trying to register on what type of women she was? The Pubs were closed and there was a snooker club ahead of her...Roberts turned a corner.

"Alright darling!"

Amanda kept on walking regardless.

"It's a bit late to be wandering about at this time of night!"

Still she ignored the stranger. Amanda was now ten metres away from Good Mews. She looked at the complex where she could see balconies on every floor. Miss Roberts entered onto its car park to get to the front door. She used the key to get into the building and could see an elevator directly ahead of her. Along the hallway, there were *Aloa Vera* plants in big vases against the walls. She proceeded onwards and nothing seemed out of the ordinary as she called for it.

"Good evening, mad'am."

Amanda turned around and saw a security guard smiling at her.

Shit! she thought. "Good evening."

"The weather was absolutely beautiful today," he said.

She nodded. "Yes it was."

A small bell could be heard and she entered inside. Selected the floor and waited a short time. After

Amanda emerged, she saw that there wasn't anybody standing guard at Oscar's. Miss Roberts saw that his door had police tape sealed along the edges of it as she got closer. Oscar did give her his keys; she broke the seal and unlocked the door before closing it behind her. In the hallway, she considered on checking out his stuff to determine Antonis' fears. Obviously, if Miss Roberts found any form of evidence that he was trouble; she would kill him. Amanda started with the bedroom; she found his medals for serving in the army. She looked behind a dressing table and uncovered a small chest; pulled it out and inside was an old rusty colt gun. Amanda gasped that the handgun wasn't looked after properly, and placed it back. She looked inside the cupboard and there were clean clothes being carelessly laid on the floor. Roberts moved them to see anything hidden within. She discovered a discarded phone and placed it in her pocket. Amanda returned the clothes back and looked inside the bedside cabinet and saw a lot of underwear garments. She moved on to the lounge and looked under the sofa-seating and found old TV magazines. Roberts also looked behind the television but there was nothing. Amanda checked her watch and had been looking around for over ten minutes. She hurried into the kitchen before switching the light on. Roberts didn't know where to start? She left the kitchen and carried on to leave his apartment and locked the door. Amanda took the stairs and was facing the same security guard.

"You not going out for a walk are you?"

Amanda laughed. "Funny you ask." She said, "I'm just going to check on my boyfriend. He just told me that he's sick."

The guard seemed less interested about her *boyfriend.* "A gorgeous girl like you shouldn't be walking the nights just to tender to your man," he said.

"Well, I'm kind of a nurse," she said.

"And you can afford to rent an apartment here?"

She smiled. "It's my boyfriend's, he's a rich guy," she said and went on her way.

Back on the streets, she decided to take a different route to the car.

***

"I was getting a little worried about you. You've been gone a full twenty-five minutes," Oscar said.

"Well, I have been pestered by some drunks coming out of a snooker club. Then I had a security guard giving me the wink about how pretty I am."

"Oh that must be Willis," Oscar responded. "He's like that with every woman. And I mean every woman who happens to walk through."

"He thinks that I should ditch you," she said smiling.

"Oh really?"

Amanda coughed. "I got some bad news. The front door is sealed off. You've just got to do your thing."

"Is there a police presence?"

She lied, "I saw a police officer knocking around at the front."

He hummed. "I just cannot risk entering the normal way. I just got to climb up onto the second floor," he said.

"There's nothing for you to get onto that balcony. In any case, you'll be exposing yourself by climbing up the wall if anybody passes by," she said.

Oscar got out of the car. "I cannot see anything else that can be plausible. Let me do my thing," he said and took his cap.

He walked the route that Amanda was walking upon and saw some men staring at him. Oscar recognised one of them from the gym: It was Josh.

"It's you, isn't it?"

Oscar tried to pretend that he couldn't hear him.

"Oi! It is you!"

Oscar carried on walking on past the snooker club and still heard him shouting from behind. He didn't want to be recognised by anybody and thought how easy it really could be for the police. Brooks was getting nearer to Good Mews, but could still hear Josh gaining on him.

Oscar turned around. "What do you want?"

"It's me you pillock — the gym when you were working up a lot of sweat. Do you remember now?"

Oscar wouldn't respond to him.

"You haven't been to the gym for weeks. Have you gone off the idea to keep fit?"

Still he didn't answer him.

"I heard that a news editor was brutally murdered with an antique letter opener! Can you believe that? I mean what kind of person takes on a grunge and kills somebody with that?" he asked, swaggered. "I mean," he went on, "that's like taking up a butter knife and using that because one is hateful over another with a block of butter, right?"

Oscar shrugged his shoulders and tried his luck that he would be left alone. *Yes,* he thought when he heard his friends calling him over. He walked on until he was directly facing his apartment below. He looked around to see anybody was there and was relieved. As a youngster, he took up free running and knew that he could get up. There was a brown exterior wall along the complex that made him certain to succeed. Oscar took a deep breath and ran towards the apartment building; leapt to create a lift onto the brown wall. He climbed on top of it and made another jump onto a first floor balcony. Oscar only had to climb up that balcony wall onto his. When he got there, he looked under an ornament to collect his notepad and diary. He remembered Amanda telling him that the police where nearby. However, he wanted to go to his bedroom to collect his old phone. As he ventured, Brooks noticed that the kitchen light was left on. Oscar had to see who or what was in there: Nobody. Anyway, he put on his bedside lamp and searched under a pile of clothes — it wasn't there. *Who has taken my phone?* he asked himself as he searched again. Oscar could hear somebody shouting. He switched off his bedside light and froze. It didn't last long and he started to look again for his phone — checking pockets as the street lighting entered his room. Again, he heard somebody outside and the front door was getting unlocked.

"I think somebody is in the kitchen."

Oscar froze again.

"I'll call the police. They'll want to hear about this."

Oscar was bemused when he heard that the police would be called upon — not that he wanted to draw attention. He saw the tip of the torch beam searching into his bedroom, and he dropped behind his bed. He took a little look, and saw a man standing inside too. The next thing, the man switched on the main lights.

Willis joined him. "The police will be here in a jiffy. It's hard to believe that Oscar Brooks is a downright murderer. How could he do such a thing?"

His colleague replied, "You can never understand anyone these days."

"Somebody broke the seal and left the kitchen light on. Who could have been here?" Josh asked him.

"Perhaps, it's those fucking reporters. You hear so much crazy shit about them like checking celebrity bins and stuff."

"But the door was locked. Nobody could have come in here."

"True but the kitchen light was on."

Both searched around his home and saw that the balcony door was opened.

"We do have an intruder here."

Oscar had better leave in a hurry before it was too late. He got up and smiled at the two security guards. "Good evening! I'm just passing through!"

Willis held him by the arm. "How did you pass though the reception? I would have seen you." He continued, after Oscar pointed at the balcony. "There's no way anybody could've jumped so high without a ladder."

Oscar shrugged his held arm and Willis let him go. "That's exactly what I did. I leapt onto the second floor."

"I'm afraid the police want you for questioning," Willis said.

"Let me guess, it's about the murder of my editor?"

"They say that you'd fled the crime scene. They only want to remove you from their investigation."

Oscar couldn't remain being a gentleman and tried to pass through them. However, Willis tackled him and he fell onto the ground. Brooks kicked him off before he was attacked by his colleague who managed to knock off his cap.

"You're not going anywhere!" Willis said as he got up.

Oscar summed-up his escape, and he punched Willis who fell onto the floor. He got to the balcony and jumped on top of the brown wall. He turned around and saw the two men looking on in amazement.

"I'll be seeing you," Oscar joked.

Brooks went over the wall and was walking along the main road. A car pulled up in front of him and two police officers jumped out. He dashed past one and was now running towards Amanda. He had to shake them off before reaching her and slipped past the front gate onto Good Mews' car park. He could hear a car speeding by and an officer on foot asking for reinforcement. Inside the complex, he saw a payphone and went up to it.

"Amanda, can you meet me outside of Good Mews?"

"Why?"

"The police are patrolling the area to where you are now."

"Oscar, you're mad! There isn't a police car in sight," Amanda responded.

"There is one because the security called on me."

"Can we meet anywhere but there?" Amanda asked.

"Get closer to the snooker club."

"There's a guy there that I don't like—"

"Just drive past that and I'll meet you half way."

"Along the road?"

"Please, yes! I've got the notepad and diary in case you were wondering."

Oscar heard her hanging up and he walked towards the gate. He looked both ways and ran across the street and hid behind a parked van. Gradually, he felt brave enough to move again until he got to the corner of the street. Oscar ducked as he heard a car racing passed him — he couldn't tell if it was an unmarked police car. Brooks peeked around the corner and saw a stationary car with its headlights on, and was 150 yards away. Oscar turned his jacket inside out. He walked slowly towards the car. Brooks could now hear a siren; he soldiered onwards regardless. The noise screamed passed him and he could see that it was a fire engine. Still walking, he recognised the driver and climbed inside.

"What have you been doing to create so much fuss?" Amanda asked.

"I could've said the same about you."

Amanda was confused by his answer. "What is that supposed to mean? I didn't set any alarms at all."

"Oh but you did," Oscar said. "Do you remember entering my flat with my keys?"

"Well," she said, "since I was there I began looking around for that list."

Oscar gave her the notepad and dairy. "Is this what you were looking for?" he asked.

Amanda only nodded.

"You left the kitchen light on and one of the security guards got suspicious."

"And what was he doing on the second floor?" Amanda asked. "He was behind the reception."

Oscar replied, "Hell do I know? I climbed onto my balcony and I got on fine."

"So where did you hid it?" Amanda wondered.

"On the balcony," he answered.

"Wait a minute," she said frowning, "when was it my fault that the alarm was raised? All you had to do is return back here. So what were you doing?"

Oscar tried to remember her two questions but answered the latter. "I was looking for my phone which had all of my contacts," he added.

"Contacts? Have you lost your mind that all of your contacts will probably see you as a murderer? You don't have any friends whatsoever," Amanda implied.

"I think my contacts may come in handy one day. It could help us in our cause."

"And who do you want to call, the SAS?" she asked, joking too.

"You never wondered on how I've heard of the dark world, have you?"

"So tell me."

"I've a good friend since being in the British forces who became a barrister. He was your father's defence lawyer."

"He will be yours if you aren't careful," she remarked. "Why on earth will he help you?"

"He's our ticket to approach Clive Roberts, your father," he said.

Amanda shook her head and turned the car around. "I think you should be more concerned about Antonis; he will offer you his full service," Amanda said.

"May I have the courtesy of knowing what that entails?"

Amanda replied, "Sure. Antonis may have been a Bible teacher in Greece but he's also a man that believes in freeing his people." She was making a turn and carried on driving ahead. "When Clive made his revelation about the Titans, Antonis thought that he was mad. But what got Antonis' attention is that that group is deep in the heroin trade. All that I can work out is that if

Clive exposed them, it was to shake the world like never before."

"You haven't answered my question," Clive said. "How can Antonis save me?"

Amanda turned to Oscar before looking ahead on the road. "Antonis knows people who'll create you a new identity."

"I supposed that includes plastic surgery too?"

Amanda stopped her car. She was looking straight at him before shaking her fist. "You think that you're very funny, don't you? Let me tell you what I was doing at your apartment, I was looking for any clues that you're a Titan. Because if you—"

"You would have killed me!" he interjected. "You've been saying that far too many times."

"It's that Graham. He thinks that my father will be murdered in prison, doesn't he?"

Oscar touched her on the shoulder. "He was toying with us. The only reason he's still alive is because those bastards think that Clive isn't their greatest worry."

"True. Antonis believes that you're their greatest concern since convincing one of them to meet up with you in Crete."

Oscar held her by the hand and she looked into his brown eyes. He could make out a single teardrop running down her face and he wiped it. "Your father is a great example who believes in righteousness. Whatever he was trying to get to the bottom of, we will succeed."

Amanda placed a hand on his lips and she was about to move forward that she heard a knock on the car window. She turned away from him to the distraction. A man was dancing outside shouting that Arsenal will be the new champions of Europe! Amanda with Oscar laughed at him before she decided to drive back to Roxy's.

"I'll tell Antonis about the list in the morning," she said.

Oscar just hummed. "It's great to fight for a noble cause. So how are we going to infiltrate them?"

Amanda was in a good mood. "With that notepad, we'll be able to go to Greece. Of course, we'll be starting from there."

He gasped. "We start there? I swear that people were trying to kill me on a daily basis. I mean how the fuck can we fight them?"

Amanda laughed. "You haven't a clue what God's Angels is capable of doing now," she answered.

...To be continued